# Beopulf

Shuichi Hashimoto

Shumpusha Publishing

To the memory of Prof. Dr. Karl Schneider

and Prof. Dr. Tamotsu Matsunami.

Beowulf

contents

## Prologue
5

\*

## Wealhtheow
11

## Grendel
29

## Draconitas in *Beowulf*
45

## The 'Thryth-Offa Digression' in *Beowulf*
69

## A Historical Survey of *Beowulf* Studies
—From the 19th to the 20th century—
83

## Interpretation of the Line 2390b in *Beowulf*
99

\*

## Epilogue
125

## Selected Bibliography
128

©Shuichi Hashimoto

All rights reserved.  No reproduction, copy,
or transmission of this publication
may be made without written permission.

First Published in Japan 2006 by Shumpusha.
53 Momijigaoka, Nishi-ku, Yokohama  220-0044 Japan

printed in Japan

ISBN4−86110−060−7 C3098 ¥2000E

# Prologue

We have known the epic that is habitually called *Beowulf*. It is an epitome of the Old English epic. The epic itself is the only relic of Anglo-Saxon time: it is the only perfect and the longest work of art in the Anglo-Saxon literature. When we appreciate an Anglo-Saxon literary work of art, in a sense, we have to discuss the culture through very limited sources. We have to know the Zeitgeist through many sources of the time and we can know it, in most cases, only through the literary works of that age.

Since the epic is the only example of the perfect copy, we can't compare the work to other examples. In the 16th century, all the monasteries were destroyed by Henry VIII. Many of the manuscripts, at the same time, were discarded and destroyed in those days. We have just some extant examples of Anglo-Saxon literature. It is dangerous to investigate the problems of the epic with just one text. Nobody can reach the exact idea of the work of art. Many examples do not always lead us to the exact ideas, however, small numbers of examples are more dangerous. Any idea will be acceptable in this sense. Then we will have our own opinions and they are nothing but the truth. The epic, *Beowulf*, is supposed to have been composed around the 7th century. After a long period of repetition of copying the text, only one parchment text has survived. The text was copied by monks. By them the text might have been slightly changed or some elements were added that the original text did not have. It is possible and probably unavoidable. But it is not necessarily of monastic origin.

Ancient Anglo-Saxon culture has been already forgotten in our modern world. We just have some traces of Anglo-Saxon times. These traces are not enough to follow and reconstruct their culture exactly. For this reason we have to depend on another source of Mediaeval Teutonic culture: Old Icelandic myth and "saga" literature, though they are a little newer than their Anglo-Saxon cousins. In spite of this limitation, they will give us some hints to our questions. One good point of the Old Icelandic literature is that it has many texts to refer to. It shows us the series of changes in expressions, for example, for paganism through the ages. In the older days paganism was the common sense of the people. It was thoroughly accepted by the people without reluctance. However, after Christianity was introduced to northern Europe, the stages of acceptance reveal the emotional changes concerning pagan ideas. The common feeling against paganism becomes worse and worse, though people keep the pagan ideas in their background. The ideas come to be covered up and mixed up with Christianity. We can see this process in "saga" literature. In an older saga paganism is common sense but in later sagas paganism becomes the symbol of what is ugly, harsh, and loathsome. Northern Europe was late in accepting Christianity, so they left some pagan elements in their literature. They deal with the ages before and after the acceptance of Christianity. Icelandic myths and sagas are the only direct example to compare with the problems of Anglo-Saxon literature. They give us good hints for the criticism of Anglo-Saxon literature.

In my opinion Ancient Japanese culture has good hints for my research as well. Both the ancient Germans and the ancient Japanese were polytheists. It will give us good hints to us, though it does not follow that the ancient Japanese religion will provide answers from beginning to end. All ancient polytheist religions will be some help to investigate the Anglo-Saxon ideas and all primitive cultures could give us some hints. The literary work, *Beowulf*, cannot be treated only from one point of view. Then in my case the ancient Japanese culture is parallel with the ancient Germanic. And the ideas of Japanese culture are close to the ideas of Anglo-Saxon culture before the acceptance of Christianity. Any ancient culture must have common elements. Before Christianity, Anglo-Saxon culture had common respects with other ancient cultures. From time to time, both cultures show common elements to each other: it follows that enemies' offspring born from their own sisters will be their common offspring on both sides. It is the function of a peace-weaver. The ideas and functions of pagan deities have common elements, and especially the functions of the tutelary deities are close to each other. It is interesting that these two cultures did not have any intercourse. In *Beowulf*, as well, we can see elements of it.

For the Christian point of view, *Beowulf* is at the early stage of the acceptance of Christianity by the Anglo-Saxon people. The poet apparently has some knowledge of the religion. But he is neither a preacher nor does he show off his knowledge of Christianity. His knowledge is supposed to be rather restricted. Yet it is evident that he had some knowledge of the Bible: as in his allusions to the story of Cain and Abel. He knows the name of "devil." In addition he has words introduced through Christian culture, such as the Latin loan words, *candel* and *gīgant* and so forth.

However his knowledge of pagan Germanic lore must have been much superior to the knowledge of Christianity. Such knowledge is apparently Christian but it is mentioned in a pagan context. The author never mentions the name of Christ nor Mary. He never mentions any other names of the saints: St. Peter, St. Paul or any other. Although we cannot find any other names from the Bible, at the same time, it is supposed that his knowledge of Christianity is profound. We should be careful when we come to the conclusion. He is never a man of simple taste. The poet has a profound philosophy. But it is not necessarily from Christianity. The

# Prologue

Anglo-Saxons had their own profound pagan philosophy. In the following papers some elements and dimensions are treated.

In its long history Christianity has accepted pagan elements through the ages, so Christianity and paganism are mixed up almost completely. Nowadays it is hard to tell Christianity from paganism. The late period of Anglo-Saxon literature has accepted Christian elements as a main source and we can say they are devoted to the Christian literature, dedicated completely to Christianity: the works of Ælfric, Wulfstan and Cynewulf.

At the root of the arguments of this small book is *Sophia Lectures on Beowulf* by Prof. Karl Schneider, from Münster University, West Germany. In my first year at the graduate school Prof. Schneider came to Japan and we were given a chance to attend a series of lectures on *Beowulf*. I am thankful and it was fortunate. The achievement of Prof. Schneider is beyond my ability and his works are voluminous in German. The lectures were series of amazing experiences that changed my point of view and even my life. His lectures were the starting point of my *Beowulf* study. In the evolving of the debate, the main point of the lectures was the relationship between Christianity and paganism in *Beowulf*. It was an inspiring and overwhelming experience for an innocent student. The debate of my papers tends to assess pagan, pre-Christian elements. The myopic access of my argument is my fault. As time has passed since the papers were printed, the assumption of my writings is supposed to let readers grin for my folly and this book may seem quaint. But let me say this is a phenomenon that has occurred to one human mind. Hopefully, this book is accepted by *Beowulf*-readers into their library and kept as long as possible.

And finally I am grateful to all the people for their help and support to continue my study and to publish my papers.

# Wealhtheow

In Old Germanic Literature women characters are given a certain important position. This is found in the *Niebelungen Lied* and Icelandic sagas. The heroines are represented as blood-thirsty characters in the works. In the rise and fall of the Scylding dynasty there seems to be a function of Wealhtheow not as a shadowy character but as the queen of destruction. The aim of this chapter is to explore the identity of Wealhtheow in *Beowulf* through the works of old Germanic literary works.

## I The etymology of Wealhtheow

Wealhtheow is a vague character. She is given a rather obscure position in *Beowulf*. It seems that her name, Wealhtheow, is not her real name but her by-name: the sense of Wealhtheow is exactly a strange one.

The epic opens with the short history of the Scylding dynasty. It is traced back to the mythical or legendary period: the founder of the dynasty, Scyld Scefing, who is regarded as mythical rather than historical. The first historical king is Healfdene. His name suggests that he is half a deity and half a human being (Half-Dane). Then he comes to have four children. The text runs as follows:

> Ðæm feower bearn        forðgerīmed
> in worold wōcun,         weoroda rǣswa[n],
> Heorogār ond Hrōðgār     ond Hālga til,
> hȳrde ic þæt[...         wæs On] elan cwēn,
> Heaðo-Scilfingas         healsgebedda.[1]
>
> (ll. 59-63)

This passage introduces the names of his four children: Heorogar, Hrothgar, Halga and Onela's queen. However, since the only extant text is defective, the name of the daughter is missing. The name is also problematic. Kemp Malone considers that the missed name is Yrsa.[2] But Yrsa is also a mysterious name. The identity of Yrsa is not clear, either. Kemp Malone summarizes the story of Yrsa as follows:

> Certainly we cannot say she was a Frank, as does Olrik. Her origin will have to be determined from a study of literary monuments. Now according to Scandian story, Helgi, while in viking, one day landed on a foreign coast, found a beautiful maiden named Ýrsa and carried her off by force. He made her his wife. In other words, Ýrsa was a foreign

captive whom Helgi made his wife. The various versions differ widely among themselves, but they are agreed here, except that Snorri makes Aðils the hero of of the adventure.[3]

Here Aðils is the Swedish Eadgils in *Beowulf*. The English *scop* may have mistaken Yrsa for Healfdene's true daughter. In *Beowulf* Hrothgar laments that Halga died young and left a son, Hrothulf. She may have stayed in the Scylding court as a daughter, then she was given to a Swedish(Scilfing) prince.[4]

Hrothgar's queen, Wealhtheow, is also problematic. There is a contradiction between her name and her status as queen of Denmark. In Old English both elements of her name (*wealh* and *þeow*) suggest the state of enslavement. The primary sense of *wealh* is "Gaulish" or "foreign". Thence is derived another sense like "slave" or "servant". The second element of her name, *þeow* is also a most common word for "servant" or "slave". Thus the literal meaning of the name is "foreign slave" or "Gaulish servant". The name, Wealhtheow, sounds like a kind of nickname.

Wealhtheow is a free born woman(*frēolīc wif*, l. 615), the lady of Helmings(*ides Helminga*, l. 620) and the king's daughter (*ðēod(nes) dohtor*, l. 2174). According to *Widsith* l. 29, Helming is a king of the Wylfings (*Helm Wulfingum*). In *Beowulf* Wealhtheow is regarded as a peace-weaver between Hrothgar and the Wylfings: Hrothgar succeeded in making a peace-treaty for the murder of Heatholaf by Ecgtheow through the marriage to Wealhtheow (cf. *Beowulf*, l. 470 ff.) She is a *friðusibb* (l. 2017), which is not only her epithet but also based on a historical peace-treaty and friendship between the Danes and the Wylfings. Through these function of Wealhtheow, her name seems to be the mistake of an English poet.[5] The *Beowulf*-poet had an enormous amount of Scandinavian literary sources and for that reason he confused one name with another, though it seems that he took no notice of his mistakes. Kemp Malone comments as follows:

> We may conclude that the poet knew Ýrsa as wife of Onela, and that he did not connect her with Halga and his wife, both of whom had passed off the Danish scene early, leaving their young son to Hroðgar and his wife to foster.[6]

There are two women: Yrsa as queen of Onela and wife of Halga and Hrothgar's wife to foster Hrothulf, probably Wealhtheow. The poet does not give us a full explanation, because his contemporary audience could understand what he intended in his narration.

## II Wealhtheow and Yrsa

The Scylding queen, Wealhtheow, is generally regarded as "poor Wealhtheow", and mistakenly trusts the treacherous

Hrothulf. He is the very person who is suspected to have killed Hrothgar and his prince, Hretheric. On their temporary good relationship the poet says as follows:

|  | Sele hlīfade |
| --- | --- |
| hēah ond horngēap; | heaðowylma bād, |
| lāðan līges; | ne wæs hit lenge þā gēn, |
| þæt se ecghete | āþumswēoran |
| æfter wælnīðe | wæcnan scolde. |

(ll. 81-85)

This passage suggests the battle between Hrothgar and his son-in-law. Hrothgar must have fought against Hrothulf in this battle. Another passage says as follows:

|  | þǣr þā gōdan twēgen |
| --- | --- |
| sǣton suhtergefæderan; | þā gȳt wæs hiera sib ætgædere, |
| ǣghwylc ōðrum trȳwe. |  |

(ll. 1163b-65)

This passage seems to imply a battle in the future, which brought the Scylding dynasty to an end. But at this moment, the narrator says, Hrothgar and Hrothulf are faithful to each other. In such a situation the queen, Wealhtheow, tries to give support to Hrothulf. Her insistence on Hrothulf may reveal her political ignorance. Her deeds have been seen to appeal indirectory to the Danish prince to refrain from the treachery that would lead the Danes to destruction.[7] The narrator gives Wealhtheow's speech as follows:

                                    Spræc ðā ides Scyldinga:
'Onfōh þissum fulle,       frēodrichten mīn,
sinces brytta!                   Þū on sǣlum wes,
goldwine gumena,          ond tō Gēatum spræc
mildum wordum,            swā sceal man dôn!
Bēo wið Gēatas glæd,      geofena gemyndig,
nēan ond feorran            þū nū hafast.
Mē man sægde,              þæt þū ðē for sunu wolde
hereri[n]c habban.            Heorot is gefælsod,
bēahsele beorhta;           brūc þenden þū mōte
manigra mēdo,              ond þīnum māgum lǣf
folc ond rīce,                 þonne ðū forð scyle,
metodsceaft seôn.          Ic mīnne can
glædne Hrōþulf,            þæt hē þā geogoðe wile
ārum healdan,               gyf þū ǣr þonne hē,
wine Scildinga,              worold oflǣtest;
wēne ic þæt hē mid gōde   gyldan wille
uncran eaferan,             gif hē þæt eal gemon,
hwæt wit tō willan         ond tō worðmyndum
umborwesendum ǣr      ārna gefremedon.'

(ll. 1168-87)

This passage sounds a little ironical. Hrothulf is Hrothgar's nephew related to her only by marriage between them.[8] As a "possible explanation" Damico speaks of her as follows: "the queen is sponsoring Hrothulf not as permanent ruler of Denmark, but as a temporary one until the princes attain maturity". However she continues: "Yet there is no substantive or formal indication in the speech to suggest that the queen regards the youngsters as future rulers or kings; rather the opposite seems to be the case."[9] From ll. 1176-80, Wealhtheow mentions that Heorot is purged;"...enjoy while you may many rewards, and leave folk and kingdom when you shall pass away, you see your death." Then just after this passage Wealhtheow mentions Hrothulf: "mīnne...glædne Hrōthulf, ll. 1180-81). This expression may be a political appeal to Hrothulf, though Wealhtheow's political intention seems to be clear. Also in ll. 1182b-83, Wealhtheow says as follows: "gyf þū ǣr þonne hē, / wine Scildinga, worold oflǣtest" (if you leave the world before him.) The ambiguity of this passage seems to reveal something intended: these lines suggest an implict intimacy and a plausible relationship between Wealhtheow and Hrothulf.

The audience may have known the implied sense in these lines. In this context, it is clear that Wealhtheow and Hrothulf have a certain hidden alliance. Wealhtheow asks Hrothgar to leave his kingdom to his kinsmen, when he must go to his destiny. Just after these words she says: "I know my friendly Hrothulf will hold the young retainers". This may mean he will rule the Danes with precedence over Hrothgar's princes, Hretheric and Hrothmud.[10] Her words sound rather ironical and suggestive. She is a shadowy woman but, considered in connection with Hrothulf, she has a certain position, though still shadowy, in *Beowulf*.

Hrothulf, as well, is a rather mysterious character. According to Damico, the introduction of Hrothulf is a little queer, for his father's name is not mentioned in the epic. Damico comments as follows:

> The poet, in fact, avoids associating the Danish prince with either of his parents. This is an oddity in the poem, since epithets expressing specific lineage are given to even the most minor characters: Aeschere is *Yrmenlāfes yldra brōþor* 'Yrmenlaf's elder brother'; Wulf is *sunu Wonrēdes* 'son of Wonred' (*Bwf* 1324, 2971). Hrothulf is denied this heroic convention. When first introduced, he is coupled with Hrothgar as *māgas* 'kinsmen', a relationship specifically defined subsequently by the term *suhtergefæderan* 'nephew-uncle'….Except for these joint circumlocutions, no other epithet denoting family ties is attached to the Danish prince.[11]

Hrothulf's father is Halga, though he is not denoted as 'Halga's son, Hrothulf' and also his mother is not mentioned. If this omission is intentional, there must be some good reason. There are two possibilities: 1) the audience have already known the names; 2) the narrator wanted to omit the names. This is because there was a rumour of incest concerning Hrothulf's mother in Old Norse literature.

Yrsa appears as king Helgi's "daughter-queen" in many Scandinavian sagas. Yrsa is assumed to be Helgi's (Halga in OE) sister, but there is a tendency in Old Norse sagas to substitute a father-daughter relationship for the one between a brother and a sister.[12] Damico summarizes the episode of the Helgi-Yrsa relationship as follows: "In Scandinavian versions of the Scylding legend, Helgi, unaware of the relationship, was enamored of his daughter, Yrsa, whom he abducted while on a viking expedition and later made his queen".[13] Though it is impossible to ascertain to what extent the narrator tells us the true state of affairs, with allusion to the legendary sources, in Old Norse literary sources Yrsa is Helgi's daughter-queen. But in *Beowulf* Yrsa is regarded as Halga's sister. It is interesting that the Scandinavian "father-daughter relationship" is turned into "brother-sister relationship". The *Beowulf*-poet, whether mistakenly or not, likes to change one name into another. In the Sigemund episode (ll. 867-97), the author substitutes Sigrðr for Sigemund. In Old Norse legend Sigemund is known for his incest with his sister, Signy. From the affair he got a son Sinfjotli (OE, Fitela). On the other hand, the episode of Sigemund is substituted for that of Sigrðr, who is known as Sigemund's second son and dragon-slayer.

Thus it is possible that the poet confuses Hrothgar's queen with Halga's widow in Heorot. Or Hrothgar may have recaptured his brother's widow. The narrator is silent about the legendary circumstances, because he and his audience may have known what happened before Beowulf came to Heorot. On the confusion of Yrsa's function Damico comments as follows:

> In all the Scandinavian sources Yrsa owes allegiance to both the Danish and the Swedish royal houses. As wife of Athils, she is ruler of the palace at Uppsala; as wife and widow of Helgi, she is queen of Denmark. If Yrsa is considered as the "missing princess" of line 62, this dual allegiance would apply in *Beowulf*, although in the southern text Yrsa would appear as the wife of the Swedish Onela and the sister of Helgi, and only through extratextual association as Helgi's wife and widow. Wealhtheow, too, holds loyalty to two separate dynasties. As Hrothgar's consort, she is *ides Scyldinga* and reigns over the magnificent Danish hall, while as *ides Helminga*, she is kindred with Wylfings, a dynasty which archeologists tend to see as a branch of the royal house of Uppsala (see Chap.4, n.28, p.210). It should be remembered, moreover, that through front variation of her name, Wealhtheow is connected with both Ecgtheow (whom Malone identifies as a Wylfing) and Ongentheow, the Scylfing king.[14]

According to Old Norse literature, Yrsa is connected with both the Swedish and Danish dynasties. In *Beowulf* Wealhtheow is called *ides Scyldinga* (Scylding lady)[15] and her other epithet is *ides Helminga* (Helming lady). As noted previously, in line 29 of *Widsith* there is *Helm Wulfingum*: Helm, the king of the Wylfings. Helming is the name of a nation, as well. The Helmings are a tribe that lived at Uppsala in Sweden. If Wealhtheow is another name of Yrsa, it is possible that Wealhtheow is Halga's widow. Then if so, she is Hrothulf's mother, but in *Beowulf* she is regarded as his aunt. This is not only a mistake by the *Beowulf*-poet but also there seems to be some intention by the author.

## III Wealhtheow's identity

In the Scadinavian Scylding saga (*Skjöldunga saga*), Helgi, being unconscious of the relationship, captured his daughter, Yrsa, on a viking raid and later made her his queen. The motif of incest is not rare even in *Beowulf*. In ll. 1931-62 the Modthryth episode has an incestuous element. Sinfrêa is the father of Modthryth, but the poet alludes to the possibility that her indication of murder excludes the implicit relationship between father and daughter. As formerly noted, the *Beowulf*-poet confuses Sigemund, the father of Fitela, with Sigrðr. The absence of reference seems to demonstrate the poet's hesitation to mention the incestuous relationship in Sigemund-Fitela episode. The poet succeeds in excluding the legendary incestuous elements from the narrative. If he had been able to dispense with Yrsa, he would have done so. But she is deeply rooted in the Scylding legend, her presence is inescapable. The poet cannot help cloaking her in obscurity.[16] In any society, incest is disgusting, so the author wanted to avoid dealing with the theme openly. By making Hrothgar extremely aged, he succeeded in hiding the implied theme enigmatically.[17] Then he could depict Wealhtheow as a shadowy but gracious queen of the Scyldings.

The *Beowulf*-poet availed himself of the rich stock of the Germanic heroic legends. The epic itself is evidence of the narrator's knowledge. He did not originate the epic and did not invent any character except Beowulf but reshaped and supplied an entertainment to his audience.

In the Old Norse saga, *Hrolfsagakraka*, and *Beowulf*, some similarity can be found between Yrsa and Wealhtheow. The two queens are united through the motif of bondmaids who rise to the status of queens: both are "foreign slaves" or *karls dottir* (peasant's daughter), who have developed into well-known queens.[18] At the same time, the queen's role as aunt-mother to Hrothulf (or Hrolf in Old Norse) is the only one point of similarity between the compositions of *Beowulf* and *Hrolfsagakraka*. It is interesting to find some similarities between Yrsa and Wealhtheow. Even after Wealhtheow gave birth to Hrothgar's two princes, Hretheric and Hrothmund, the implicit relationship shows her as surrogate mother to Hrothulf. Thus there is some indication that as Sisam indicates, Hrothulf was a famous warrior by his valor and Hrethric was notorious for his ill-nature.[20] Even if there is some good reason for Wealhtheow, it is anomalous that she could show preference for Hrothulf, her nephew, over Hrothgar's offspring. The possibility arises that Wealhtheow is aunt-mother to Hrothulf, as Yrsa to Hrolf. If Wealhtheow is mother to Hrothulf, Wealhtheow's equivocal conduct of faith and affection to her nephew becomes comprehensible as a satisfactory explanation. In addition to this extratextual evidence, it is possible that Wealhtheow and Hrothulf (or Hrolf) descend from a common poetic source and share a mutual legendary heritage. According to *Ynglinga saga*, Hrolf is recognized as chief of the Wylfings: Wealhtheow's tribe.[21] Although Wealhtheow is enigmatic, if Wealhtheow's literary identity is that of Yrsa as Helgi's widow and Hrolf's mother, here comes out a possibility that Wealhtheow promoted the murder of Hrothgar and his prince which was undertaken by Hrothulf. She is a shadowy character even in the murder of the Scyldings, but her words imply that she is the promoter of the feud behind the textual evidence. In Old Germanic literature, a woman whose family member was killed will often promote the feud against her enemy. As formerly noted, in *Volsunga saga*, Signy exhausted all her sons by her husband, then she finally gave birth to Sinfjotli by her brother, Sigemund. This is because all her sons were cowards for the purpose of vengeance. So she had incest with her brother. After they completed their vengeance, she committed suicide. In the latter part of the *Niebelungen Lied*, the theme of the epic turns into the heroine's vengeance against Hagen, the murderer of her erstwhile husband. For her purpose she remarried Attila of the Huns and utilized his army for genocide. In other Old Norse literary works, as well, women characters become more eager to take revenge than other male characters. In some texts of the *Elder Edda* a heroine roasted the hearts of her children to whom she gave birth by the murderer of her former husband. Then she served the roast to the murderer: her temporary spouse.[22] The female characters in the heroic period were more wise and cruel than the male characters. It is probable that Wealhtheow utilizes Hrothulf for her long standing feud against Hrothgar. She herself was the real murderer and the destroyer of the Scylding dynasty.

## Conclusion

The major trait of characters in Old Norse and Anglo-Saxon literature is the profundity of their mind.[23] In the same sense, narrative treachery is foreshadowed in the merriment of Heorot, which refers to a battle that will exhaust Hrothgar's hall. The former part of *Beowulf* treats, so to speak, the internal affairs of the Scylding dynasty. If Hrothulf is identified as Wealhtheow's son, the queen's behaviour is explainable. Hrothulf is known for his treachery against Hrothgar, and he himself is destroyed by his close cousin, Heoroweard. On the destruction of the

Scylding dynasty, Wealhtheow and Hrothulf are conspirators in this sense. Wealhtheow is not a weak and silent woman. She incites Beowulf to fight against the Grendels. In Old Germanic literature female characters are often promoters of new fights: they exhort male characters to fight or to take vows of vengeance.

Wealhtheow is enigmatic but if she is considered as having the function of a priestess, she has a similar function to Lady Macbeth: she is depicted as a calm and gracious but under her shadowy existence she has some elements of a witch. In Old Germanic literature women could be extremely demonic: even children could be used as tools of vengeance. There are many other demonic episodes about female characters in Old Norse literary works. Women were the last ones to fight but they were the promoters of the everlasting feud. In this sense the Old Germanic women were more free than their descendants in later centuries. They were shadowy and calm but they had the potential power to exhort male-warriors to fight.

The epic, *Beowulf*, is a song of destruction: even the winners will be destroyed before long. All dynasties will come to an end. The theme of *Beowulf* tells us the undepictable sadness of the Old Germanic society.

## Notes

1. Frederick Klaeber, ed. *Beowulf and the Fight at Finnsburg* (Lexington: D.C. Heath, 1950). All quotations henceforth are from this edition.
2. Kemp Malone, "The Daughter of Healfdene," in his *Studies in Heroic Legend and in Current Speech*, ed. S. Einarsson and N.E. Eliason (Copenhagen: Rosenkilde and Bragger, 1959), p.141; Cf. Norman E. Eliason "Healfdene's Daughter," in *Anglo-Saxon Poetry: essays in appreciation* ed. Lewis E. Nicholson and Dolores Warwick Frese (Notre Dame: University of Notre Dame Press, 1975), pp.3-13.
3. Malone, p.139.
4. Malone, p.138.
5. Kemp Malone concludes that: "I take it that Wealhtheow is a nickname properly belonging to Ýrsa, and that the English poet, by mistake, applied it to the wrong daughter-in-law." p.140.
6. Malone, p.141.
7. Helen Damico, *Beowulf's Wealhtheow and the Valkyrie Tradition* (Madison: University of Wisconsin Press, 1984), p.128; Edward B. Irving Jr., *A Reading of Beowulf* (New Haven: Yale University Press, 1968), p.141.
8. Damico, p.127.
9. Damico, p.127.
10. Kenneth Sisam, *The Structure of Beowulf* (Oxford: Clarendon Press, 1966), pp.35-36; Sisam gives an idea that Hrothulf is a glorious hero. He comments as follows: "Yet in all sources, early and late, he is a character to be admired. He appears in the post-Conquest list of heroes popular among the English which Imelmann discovered in MS. Vespasian D iv. Scandinavian traditions agree in making him the best and most glorious of early Danish kings." p.36.
11. Damico, pp. 110-111.

12. Damico, p.92; Cf. Damico, ibid., p.116.
13. Damico, p.92.
14. Damico, pp.120-121; Cf. Johannes Hoops, *Kommentar zum Beowulf* (Heidelberg: Carl Winter, 1965), p.153.
15. On the details of *ides*, see Jane Chance, *Women as Hero in Old English Literature* (Syracuse: Syracuse University Press, 1986), pp.1-12.
16. Damico, p.176.
17. Sisam, p.35.
18. Damico, p.172.
19. Damico, p.132.
20. Sisam, p.38.
21. Snorri Sturluson, *Ynglinga Saga*, trans. Lee M. Hollander, in *Heimskringla: History of the Kings of Norway* (Austin: University of Texas Press, 1991), p.40.
22. Teiji Yoshimura, *Geruman Shinwa* (Tokyo: Yomiuri Sinbunsha, 1972), pp.128-133; *Edda*, trans. Yukio Taniguchi (Tokyo: Shinchosha, 1973), pp.175-195.
23. Damico, p.90.

# Grendel

## I

þyrs sceal on fenne gewunian/ana inna lande (=The giant must inhabit in wasteland, alone in the land.)[1]

This is how an Anglo-Saxon proverb defines the giant. Indeed, the Anglo-Saxons believed in these demons, and in *Beowulf* we find one such giant moor stalker: the notorious Grendel.

Grendel is described in various ways: as a giant (*þyrs*, l. 426, *eoten*, l. 761), an enemy in hell (*fēond on helle*, l. 101), a bold demon (*ellengǣst*, l. 86) and a fierce visitor (*grimma gǣst*, l. 102), and these nominations all suggest the characteristics of a demon. Though he was bigger than any other man (*he wæs māra þonne ænig man oðer*, l. 1353), he is in man's form (*on weres wæstmum*, l. 1352). Grendel is depicted as an unhappy man (*wonsǣlī wer*, l. 105), and a wight of evil (*wiht unhǣlo*, l. 120). Grendel has a spirit as well as a body: *ālegde, hǣþene sāwle; þǣr him hel onfēng* (gave up heathen soul; then hell took him, ll. 851-852).[2] Grendel is called *āglǣca* (monster, warrior, l. 159) or *rinc* (man, warrior, l. 720). And Beowulf, as well, is called in the same epithet (*āglǣca*, l. 893, *rinc*, l. 747). They are treated as warriors in the epic.

This paper is an attempt to explore the true identity of Gendel: how the monster symbolizes human history; why he comes to be regarded as a monster.

## II

In ll. 100-114, the monster, Grendel, first appears in the epic. He was a fierce demon, prescribed in Cain's kin. He is a notorious wanderer, who possesses moors, fens and a stronghold. Then after the construction of Heorot he painfully endured the mirth in the hall.

On the figure of Grendel, F. Klaeber regards it as "originally an ordinary Scandinavian troll" but also "as an impersonation of evil and darkness, even an incarnation of the Christian devil."[3] Grendel is not only Cain's kin, but also *fyrena hyrde* (keeper of sins, l. 750), *fēond mancynnes* (enemy of mankind, l. 164), and *Godes andsaca* (God's enemy, l. 786, l. 1682). The some idea is expressed in: *hǣþen* (heathen, l. 852, l. 986). Same scholars seem to be aware that Grendel may symbolize a human being, and among others J.R.R. Tolkien remarks as follows:

> Their parody of human form (*earmsceapen on weres wæstmum* [the miserable creature in the form of a man]) becomes symbolical, explicitly, of sin, or rather this mythical element, already present implicit and unresolved, is emphasized: this we see already in *Beowulf*, strengthened by the theory of descent from Cain (and so from Adam), and of the curse of God. So Grendel is not only under this inherited curse, but also himself sinful:....[4]

Tolkien submits his insight into the nature of Grendel. Grendel is known to be as under Cain's curse. But his human form is the cause of distress: he is a monster in a human form.

### III

The period of the production of *Beowulf* is the age when the Christian missionaries were struggling against the Germanic ethic, such as, bloodrevenge.[5] Anglo-Saxon Christians accepted the legend of Cain, and the *Beowulf*-poet employed it not as a theological myth but as a literary legend.[6]

Probably the Christian missionaries explained their teachings to the primitive Anglo-Saxons in terms of the Germanic legendary sources.[7] William Whallon says: "A missionary may have taught the poet only what could be combined with the native heroic ideals, and *Beowulf* may reflect the felicity of the combination."[8] It might be easier for the Anglo-Saxons to believe that human beings had been cursed because the first man's son had committed fratricide. Whallon remarks how popular the story of Cain was among the Christians:

> For Augustine, toward the beginning of Book XII of the *Contra Faustum*, discoursed extensively upon the underlying meanings of the story of Cain, and many of other Fathers did likewise, so that it was and is impossible to mention Cain without potentially invoking the patrology for elucidation.[9]

The story of Cain must have been popular, because fratricide was not uncommon among the Anglo-Saxons. Even from *Beowulf*, some examples may be gathered: Hroðgar might have killed his brother, Unferð is said to have murdered his brothers, and the Swedish king, Onela, killed his brother to get the Swedish throne.[10]

All the mediaeval monsters could be accepted in the theological system of Christianity by considering that the demons are descended from Cain.[11] Grendel may have historical profundity deduced from the name of Cain. Through the idea that Grendel was prescribed in Cain's kin, the author might have wanted to add some biblical elements in the epic for the Christian audience.[12]

## IV

Michael Alexander comments: "In Scandinavia Grendel was a troll, but in Christian England he belongs to the kindred of Cain:"[13] Certainly Grendel and his mother are called *dēofla* (l. 1680) and Grendel, in fleeing to his hiding place, is seeking *dēofla gedræg* (devils' company, l. 756), but according to Tolkien, "The changes which produced (before A.D. 1066) the medieval devil are not complete in *Beowulf* but in Grendel change and blending are, of course, already apparent."[14] Grendel is primarily "a physical monster"[15] who is "slain by plain prowess."[16] He has a mortal body which is to be destroyed by a hero.

While Grendel is *þyrs* or *eoten* (giant) and of *fifelcyn* (race of monsters), his commonest epithet is simply an enemy: *lāð, fēond, sceaða, laðgetēona, feorhgenīðla*. Tolkien observes that all these words are appropriate to "enemies of any kind."[17] Also several epithets referring to his "*outlawry*"[18] are applied to him. J.B. Baird defines "Grendel's *condition* as man-exile."[19] He considers that Grendel is exiled not only "by God" but also "by man."[20]

It may be said that the story of Grendel is a historical legend in the motif of a monster against the city walls.[21] The mediaeval city represents the contrast between its walls and the wilderness into which criminals were driven.[22] In this sense, Cain is an outsider; Adam and the other descendants of his are insiders.[23] The demon, as a descendant of Cain, is an exile from human society. Baird points out Grendel's two dimensions: "monster and man, Christian demon and heathen outlaw."[24] Grendel's two dimensions are unavoidable.

Many people have lost their estate and property through warfare, and refugees could not help finding their dwelling place in wasteland. Such outsiders came to be regarded as monsters and demons. Grendel may symbolize such expelled people, and people must have fought to get back their property. Such fights were common among the Anglo-Saxon or Germanic society. Grendel's attack against Heorot may symbolize their rearguard action against the Scyldings. And *Dryhten* (lord, l. 108) that prescribed Grendel is not necessarily Christian God that could be the tutelary deity of the Scyldings. When we investigate the genealogy of the Scyldings. When we investigate the genealogy of the Scyldings in ll. 4-63, the details of the family line becomes as follows:

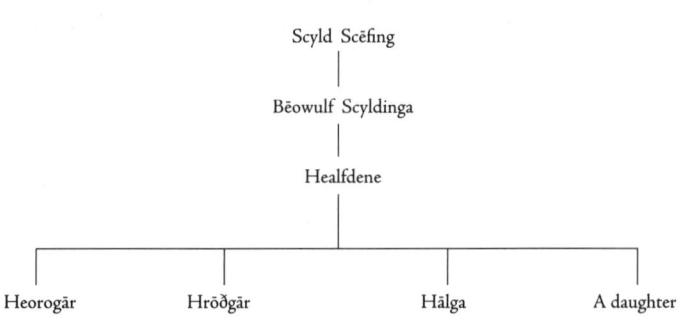

```
                    Scyld Scēfing
                         |
                   Bēowulf Scyldinga
                         |
                      Healfdene
                         |
    ┌────────────┬───────────────┬──────────────┐
 Heorogār    Hrōðgār           Hālga        A daughter
```

We find the name of Scyld Scēfing. His name signifies: "Scyld, the son of Scēf." Scēf is the begetter of Scyld and Scyld's son is Bēowulf Scyldinga. He is usually called Beowulf I to distinguish between him and Beowulf of the Geats. Then we find the name of Healfdene who has three sons and a daughter: Heorogār, Hrōðgār, Hālga, and a daughter whose name is unknown.

Healfdene, the ancestor of the Scyldings, can be analytically recognized as "half-Dane." His name indicates that his father is a god and his mother is a Danish woman. He is called after his human feature.[25]

Here we should returen to Scyld Scēfing. As previously noted, Scēf is the begetter of Scyld. Karl Schneider introduces the Scēfmyth by Æthelweard and from the *Gesta Regum Anglorum* of William Malmesbury:

> Sleeping in a boat on a sheaf and surrounded by weapons Scēf as a small boy is washed ashore on a beach of Scandinavia. There he finds foster parents, grows up and is finally made king. With him (and now according to the *Beowulf* passage) a long sovereignless period of great suffering comes to an end. Scēf during his reign becomes a powerful king of his people, who subdues all tribes at the borders of his empire and makes them tributaries. After his death he is laid out on a ship together with rich treasures. Then the ship is left to the waves without helmsman.[26]

J. Hoops comments that the Scyld episode in *Beowulf* is as same as what Æthelweard and William of Malmesbury report.[27] The similar episode is found in the 22nd stanza of the Old English *Runename Poem*:

> Ing among the East-Danes was first/ beheld by men, until that later time when to the east/ he made his departure over the wave, followed by his chariot;/ that was the name those stern warriors gave the hero.[28]

From outside of England plentiful evidence has been reported about the god: Ing. In *Germania* Tacitus informs a Germanic tribe, Ingaevones, who were the followers of the god: *Inguaz. And in the Old Norse Snorri Sturlusson notes that the god, Freyr, is also called Yngvi or Yngvifreyr: the Freyr of Ing. And in *Ynglinga Saga* his descendants are called Ynglingar.

The name, Scyld, means "shield" that can be understood as a protector in battle. Through this function this name is identical with the name, Gārmund: "protector by means of a spear."[29] Here we should remember the Offa genealogy in the Mōdprȳð episode(ll. 1931-1962). According to the *Beowulf* text, the genealogy comes to be as follows:

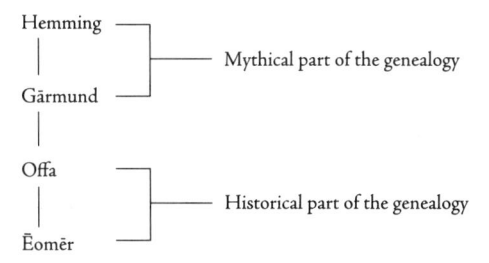

```
Hemming ┐
   |    │
   |    ├──── Mythical part of the genealogy
Gārmund ┘
   |
   |
Offa    ┐
   |    ├──── Historical part of the genealogy
Ēomēr   ┘
```

Gārmund is the offspring of the god, Hemming. Through the function as a protector in battle, two names, Gārmund and Scyld are identical. Karl Schneider remarks: "In *Beowulf* the myth has been shifted from father to son."[30] Here we know that Scēf is Scyld's begetter, and Beowulf I and Scēf are identical. Schneider comments on this point as follows:

> In the light of religious history Scēf (or Scēafa—i.e."(the one belonging to the) sheaf"—)resp. Bēow (or Bēowa—i.e."(the one belonging to )barley"—)are identical with the Anglo-Saxon pagan god of the earth, usually called Ing(i.e. the begetter).[31]

In Schneider's idea Scēf and Bēow are identical. And they denote the fertility god, Ing, as well. He is the begetter of his progeny and also he is the devine ancestor of the Scylding dynasty.

So the genealogy of the Scylding dynasty derived from the other testimony comes to be as follows:[32]

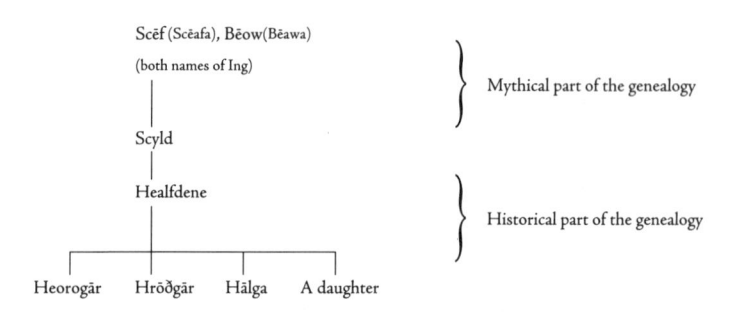

```
Scēf(Scēafa), Bēow(Bēawa)
(both names of Ing)              ⎫
                                 ⎬  Mythical part of the genealogy
Scyld                            ⎭
│
Healfdene                        ⎫
                                 ⎬  Historical part of the genealogy
┌──────┬──────┬──────┐           ⎭
Heorogār  Hrōðgār  Hālga  A daughter
```

Ing is the ancestor of the dynasty. The other appellations of the Scyldings are *Dene* (Danes) and *Ingwine* (Ing's friends, l. 1044, l. 1319). The name *Ingwine* indicates that they are the people under the protection of the god: Ing. From this point of view, in the context of ll. 100-114, the words, *Scyppend*, *Dryhten* or *Metod*, could be the tutelary deity for the Scyldings. And the names of the deity should be led to the Primary Being that is common among the Germanics.[33] We should remember that the characters in the epic are living in the pagan world.

Fred C. Robinson comments as follows:

> When Beowulf and his Geatisc companions complete their voyage to Denmark, we are told, "Gode þancedon/ þæs þe him yþlade eaðe wurdon" (227-28). And the modern editors' invariable practice of capitalizing the first letter of *Gode* creates the problem so often remarked by critics: how could pagan Geatas pray to the Christian God? But

when we turn to the original, uncapitalized form of the manuscript, we can translate the sentence, "They gave thanks to a god for the fact that the ocean journey had been an easy one." That is the meaning of the sentence in the context of the pagan world inhabited by the characters in the poem.[34]

The author fully utilizes the ambiguity of the context. This is the poet's favorite technique. It seems that he slides his intention into the context. We can see elsewhere the double meaning of the god.[35] In *Beowulf* the author must have been obliged to utilize the ambiguity in the context of his work.

## Conclusion

Here we have seen the features of the monster, Grendel. Through the tactics of the Christian missionaries, the story of Cain and Abel may have become popular among the Christians. The primitive Anglo-Saxons may have had a background to accept the idea of the original sin through the story of Cain.

The episode of Grendel may have the historical and cultural background in terms of the motif of the monster against the city walls: the demon is the outsider of the human society. Grendel could represent the human beings who were expelled through the warfare with the Scyldings.

In short, Grendel was exiled by the tutelary deity of the Scyldings: the god, Ing. The *Beowulf*-poet could not help utilizing ambiguity. He was the man who was in the age of pagans and Christians existing together.[36]

In this short paper we could not investigate the other features of the Grendels: he and his mother are invulnerable against weapons. He is said, "*he sigewæpnum forsworen hæfde*" (he laid a spell on victorious weapons, l. 804). He is *helrūnan* (warlock, l. 163). Further, in Grendel's abode Beowulf fortunately finds a giant's sword. Grendel's mother is also invulnerable against the sword: Hrunting. These features seem to suggest the other elements of the Grendels. In brief, they might have the craft of weapon-making.[37] In Old Norse mythology, dwarfs are considered as blacksmiths. The mythical blacksmith, Wēland, is well known in Old Norse and Old English literature. There might be some relationship between the Grendels and these legendary blacksmiths.

---

## Notes

* I am much dependent on Prof. Dr. Karl Schneider. The remaining inadequicies in argumentation are my responsibility.
1. MS. Cotton Tibelius. B.i.; Maxims II, 41-42. Elliot Van Kirk Dobbie (ed.): *The Anglo-Saxon Minor Poems* The Anglo-Saxon Poetic Records VI (New York: Columbia University Press, 1942), p.56.
2. J.R.R. Tolkien, "*Beowulf*: The Monsters and the Critics," in *Anthology*

*of Beowulf Criticism* ed. Lewis E. Nicholson (Notre Dame, Indiana: University of Notre Dame Press, 1980), p.89.
3. Frederick Klaeber, *Beowulf and the Fight at Finnsburg*, 3rd ed. (Lexington: D.C. Heath and Company, 1950), p.1.
4. Tolkien, ibid., p.89.
5. David Williams, *Cain and Beowulf; A Study in Secular Allegory* (Toronto: University of Toronto Press, 1982), p.10; Karl Schneider, *Sophia Lectures on Beowulf*, ed. Shoichi Watanabe and Norio Tsuchiya (Tokyo: Taishukan, 1986), pp.165-166.
6. William Whallon, "The Christianity of *Beowulf*", *Modern Philology* 60 (1962/63), p.82.
7. Whallon, ibid., p.90.
8. Whallon, ibid., p.82.
9. Whallon, ibid., p.85.
10. Cf. Schneider, ibid., p.91.
11. Williams, ibid., p.32.
12. Charles Moorman, "The Essential Paganism of *Beowulf*", *Modern Language Quarterly* 28 (1967) comments:"... one must accept the fact that the audience of *Beowulf* must have been very close indeed to its pagan heritage and could still understand and appreciate in its own terms a pagan tale, even though that tale might be shaped and rendered respectable by a poet with an eye cocked toward the local clergy", (p.8).
13. Michael Alexander, *Old English Literature* (London; The MacMillan Press, 1983), p.63.
14. Tolkien, ibid., pp.88-89.
15. In other parts Tolkien indicates as follows: "Thus in spite of shifting, actually in process (intricate, and as difficult as it is interesting and important to follow), Grendel remains primarily an ogre, a physical monster, whose main function is hostility to humanity (and its frail efforts at order and art upon earth)", (p.90); Tolkien again comments:

"This approximation of Grendel to a devil does not mean that there is any confusion as to his habitation. Grendel was a fleshly denizen of this world (until physically slain)". (p.90).

16. Tolkien, ibid., p.91.
17. Tolkien, ibid., p.91.
18. Tolkien, ibid., p.91.
19. Joseph L. Baird, "Grendel the Exile", *Neuphilologische Mitteilungen* 67 (1966), p.380; Cf. Baird, ibid., p.381.
20. Baird, ibid., p.379; Cf. Baird, ibid., p.380.
21. Williams, ibid., p.47.
22. Williams, ibid., p.46.
23. Williams, ibid., p.46.
24. Baird, ibid., p.378.
25. Schneider, ibid., p.17-18.
26. Schneider, ibid., p.17.
27. Johannes Hoops, *Kommentar zum Beowulf* (Heidelberg: Carl Winter, 1965), p.5.
28. Maureen Halsall, *The Old English Rune Poem: a critical edition* (Toronto: University of Toronto Press, 1981), p.91.
29. Schneider, ibid., p.17.
30. Schneider, ibid., p.17.
31. Schneider, ibid., p.17; Karl Schneider remarks on the name Beowulf Scyldinga: "Alliteration between the names of a father and his son(s) is a characteristic feature of Old Germanic genealogies. In this genealogy, however, the name of Bēowulf does not alliterate with Scyld. Bēowulf I as a genealogical link, therefore, seems to be an error in this genealogy." (p.16).
32. Schneider, ibid., p.16.
33. Cf. Schneider, p.258
34. Fred C. Robinson, *Beowulf and the Appositive Style* (Knoxville: The University of Tennessee Press, 1985), p.40.

35. Robinson, ibid., p.69.
36. Robinson, ibid., p.30; Cf. Whallon, ibid., p.82.
37. Howell D. Chickering Jr. *Beowulf: A Dual-Language Edition* (Garden City, NY: Anchor Books, 1977), p.343; To this idea there is another point of view: it is possible that giants do not imply the fabulous beings but the historical human beings who had had far more advanced civilization than the Germanic people, that is, the Romans. When the Romans invaded the lands of the Teutonics, they brought their own civilization. And for the Germanic people the most important heritage was the swords made with better technique. The Roman swords must have been quite strong and tough. So for the Germanic people such swords must have had some fabulous and magical power. Then they came to believe that the swords had been made by the giants. In *Beowulf* we find some reference to the giants but these giants might be some ancient people who had lived in the former time. Likewise the treasure guarded by the dragon is called the works of the giants: "Ða ic on hlæwe gefrægn hord rēafian, / eald enta geweorc ānne mannan," (ll. 2773-4)(=Then I heard of the hoard plunder in a cave, old giant's works through a certain man). Cf. Hiroshi Fujiwara, "Yaiba mote Tsuyoki Inishie no Tsurugi", Off-printed from *The Annual Collection of Essays and Studies*, Faculty of Letters, Gakushuin University, Vol. XXXII(1985), pp.25-35.

# Draconitas in *Beowulf*

Draca sceal on hlæwe,/frod, frætwum wlanc.[1]
(*Maxims* II, ll. 26-27)

The third enemy that Beowulf encounters is symbolically the most mysterious demon. Considering his manifestation solely in the view of the whole European literature, though he is so popular in human imagination, he is of all the monsters the most universally accepted. As to the characteristics of the dragon David Williams explains as follows:

> Throughout medieval tradition the dragon was interpreted as the Devil in monster guise, based upon the form that Satan adopted to seduce Eve. In this manifestation he is Leviathan, and the symbol is expressive not of generalized evil but of a malice more particular. Whether it be Ladon or the Beast of the Apocalypse, the evil dragon is identified with time and the disruption of order.[2]

In the mediaeval tradition, the dragon was, naturally, the Satan "in monster guise." He was nothing but a devil and the symbol of evil in human imagination. At the same time he is considered as the being that is "twice condemned": he is regarded as "a form of Satan" and is "in further preventing the conversion of the treasure to redemptive purposes by hoarding it, he is considered an enemy of progress and knowledge."[3] However much the dragon is considered as the devil, there seems to turn up some question about the interpretation of the dragon in *Beowulf*. The aim of this paper is to consider the identity of the dragon in *Beowulf*: whether the dragon be a devil or some other being that it represents or symbolizes in the Anglo-Saxon period.

I

As in the *Anglo-Saxon Maxims* II, the dragon is believed to exist in the real world as a physical monster. In ll. 2824-35 of *Beowulf*, the dragon is described as a mortal creature. He is not an abstruct being. Even the fire which the dragon blows was not unreasonable for educated people in the eighth century: "This material at any rate confirms that the association snake-venom-chemical heat-fire seemed reasonable to men of learning in the eighth century."[4] As A.K. Brown remarks of the dragon in Old English documentaries:

> A Latin annal parallel to the Old English one for 793 adds

"fiery strokes" to the Chronicle's "enormous lightnings and fiery dragons flying through the air": *fulmina abominanda et dracones per aera igneique ictus saepe vibrare et volitare videbantur.* This might be a conflation as well as a translation of the Old English annal, since if the words corresponding to it are removed, the remaining phrase *ignei ictus...saepe vibrare* is an obvious improvement in wording which would provide the more sober Latin equivalent to the English "firedrake." This seems to be the case in two earlier eighth-century Latin entries, where *ignei ictus* portend the deaths of important churchmen and the deposition of a king, since the earlier entry, A.D. 744, has a vernacular equivalent in the Anglo-Saxon Chronicle, *steorran foran swyðe scotienda*, i.e. there were remarkable shooting stars, while the early Irish annals for what may be the same year read *dracones in caelo visi sunt*. A few years earlier still, apparently as a presage of the Venerable Bede's death, the Irish annals record "a huge dragon seen at the end of autumn with a great thunderclap after it," *draco ingens in fine autumni cum tonitruo magno post se*, which certainly sounds diagnostic of a meteor fall.[5]

In the Old English annals the dragon appears as a portent of malicious accidents. In *The Anglo-Saxon Chronicle* the dragon is seen in the year of the first viking raid. And in Old Germanic literature the dragon reveals his feature. Hilda Ellis Davidson comments as follows:

Then after he too has died we are told that the "ancient foe of the dawn" (the dragon) "found the splendour of the hoard left open", (2271) and took possession. He brooded over the treasure for 300 years until a man badly in need of ransom money came upon it by chance and carried off a cup while the dragon slept. The account suggests that this is a rationalization of the idea (which would be repugnant to a Christian audience) that the dead man himself became a dragon. It is a familiar idea in Old Norse literature: Fafnir himself only turned into a dragon when he had gained possession of Andvari's treasure, whereupon he retired to a lair on Gnitaheath, which as described in a note to Fafnismál suggests a burial mound, and in one of the Icelandic Sagas several members of a strange family become dragons and lie on chests of gold behind a waterfall. Very interesting in this connection is the story of the tomb of Charles Martel given in several medieval chronicles. The Bishop of Orleans dreamed that Charles was in hell, and his tomb was opened, whereupon a fiery dragon darted out, leaving the tomb blackened as if burnt up. The story is found as early as 858, about a century after the incident is said to have taken place, and is vouched for by the writer, who claims to have known some of those present.[6]

The existence of the dragon was obvious for mediaeval people. Human beings can believe in what they have never seen before: we can believe in elephants, whales, and dinosaurs even before we look at them. For the *Beowulf*-poet as well, the dragon must have been something natural.

Here we should like to see the outline of the fire-dragon that is presented by Hilda Ellis Davidson:

> "Then did the visitant spit forth embers and burn up the bright dwellings; that flaming ray wrought mischief to men, for the enemy flying through the air would leave nothing alive... he had encompassed the people of the land with burning, with flame and fire" (2312-22). Beowulf tries to protect himself with a non-inflammable shield, which, however, proves less effective than he had hoped. (2337f. 2570f.). The dragon was reckoned by the Geats to be 50 ft. long (3042) when they saw it after death (the size of a large sperm whale), and it had some of the characteristics of a serpent, for the term *hring-bogan* (coiled into rings) is used of it, (2561) and the word *orm* (serpent) as often as *draca*. But it is definitely a winged creature, the "far-flier" and "night-flier"; "it had been wont to delight in the air in the night hours and come down again to seek its den." (3043-5). It had also powerful teeth, with which it dealt Beowulf his death wound. Above all it is the guardian of the burial mound:[7]

Is is interesting that the dragon is 50 ft. and Davidson indicates that it is "the size of a large sperm whale." For the Anglo-Saxons, the representative largest creature was the sperm whale. The size of 50 ft. was a reasonable length for the *Beowulf*-poet and his audience.

The characteristics of the dragon is quite simple. Once he

is settled in his lair, he has slept peacefully for 300 years, as a guard of an ancient hoard, but when a thief dares to steal in, his enormous potential of destructive power is revealed, his anger boils and he vomits fire to burn whatever he finds on his way.

He is regarded as opposite to the ideal kingship. The highest value of the Anglo-Saxon king was the sharing of the treasure or the ring distributor. Hoarding by the dragon suggests the opposition to the social system in a comitatus.[8]

J.R.R. Tolkien provides an interesting comment on the dragon in *Beowulf* as follows:

> ...but the conception, none the less, approaches *draconitas* (dragon-ness)] rather than *draco* (dragon): a personification of malice, greed, destruction (the evil side of heroic life), and of the undiscriminating cruelty of fortune that distinguishes not good or bad (the evil aspect of all life).[9]

Tolkien defines the monster not as the dragon but as *draconitas* (dragon-ness). He is not only a monster but also another side of heroic life. Tolkien considers that the dragon symbolizes the evil side of heroic life. He is the anti-hero in the epic. In the world we know as *draconitas*, there are "no names, no orderly successions, no dynasties, no society at all, none."[10] It is represented as the cold, wild and warlike atmosphere that lacks any human gentleness. The dragon is the people's, malicious foe, a fierce spotted horror, a hoard guard, a far-flier, desperate at night, and fire dragon.

## II

The dragon is so frightful and demonic but he is in some points humanized. In the point that he is a physical being, he has flesh and blood, and fights in response to an open challenge with Beowulf, so that he is killed by the sword of Wiglaf. He is given a good reason to be angry. He does not indiscriminately seek out the human society of the Geats to lay waste but because of their committing theft from the hoard which he guarded. He is fundamentally a guard (*hordweard*, l. 2293, l. 2302 and *beorges hyrde*, l. 2304). On his function as a guard Edward B. Irving Jr. comments as follows: "The rudimentary thoughts a dragon might have about treasure are the thoughts a crocodile has about a fish, though doubtless even less rational and easily explained."[11] The dragon's function as guard of a hoard seems as if it were his instinct. When he notices that he has had his golden cup stolen, his behaviour is quite similar to that of a child who misses his favorite toy. The text runs as follows:

>      Þā se wyrm onwōc,     wrōht wæs genīwad;
>      stonc ðā æfter stāne,     stearcheort onfand
>      fēondes fōtlāst;
>
>                                         (ll. 2287-89)[12]

He notices the theft and finds the footprint of the thief. The poet continues to describe the confusion of the dragon as follows:

>                              Hordweard sōhte
> georne æfter grunde,         wolde guman findan,
> þone þe him on sweofote      sāre getēode;
> hāt ond hrēohmōd             hlǣw oft ymbehwearf
> ealne ūtanweardne;
>
> (ll. 2293-97)

The dragon considers that he might have made a mistake, so that he sometimes comes back to his barrow and looks for his precious cup again. The passage, *hlǣw oft ymbehwearf ealne ūtanweardne* (ll. 2296-97), effectively represents his confusion. He is not only a dreadful being but also humanized or rather humorous.

Naturally the dragon is called a *fēond* (fiend, enemy) in l. 2706, but at the same time Beowulf and Wiglaf are also designated *fīonda* in l. 2671. They are regarded from the dragon's point of view. The *Beowulf*-poet says as follows:

> Fēond gefyldan        ——ferh ellen wræc —— ,
> ond hī hyne þā bēgen   ābroten hæfdon,
> sibæðelingas;          swylc sceolde secg wesan,
> þegn æt ðearfe!
>
> (ll. 2706-09)

This is a part of the dragon fight, the dragon is called fiend by the narrator in l. 2706. This is natural from the Geats' side. Here we should turn our eyes to that of the dragon. The text runs as follows:

> Æfter ðām wordum  wyrm yrre cwōm,
> atol inwitgæst  ōðre sīðe
> fȳrwylmum fāh  fīonda nīos(i)an,
> lāðra manna.
>
> (ll. 2669-72)

In the fighting scene, Beowulf and Wiglaf are called *fīonda* (l. 2671) and in the next line they are called *lāðra manna* (hostile men) as a variation of *fēond*.

As well as Grendel, Sigemund and Beowulf, the dragon is called an *āglǣca* (monster, warrior, hero). Grendel's mother as well, is called *āglǣca-wīf*. This indicates that these *āglǣcan* are regarded as awesome warriors. In l. 2592, Beowulf and the dragon are called, in the plural form, *āglǣcan*. The text runs as follows:

> Næs ðā long tō ðon,
> þæt ðā āglǣcean  hȳ eft gemētton
>
> (ll. 2591-92)

In these lines Beowulf and the dragon are regarded as warriors of awful strength from the viewpoint of the poet.

Also they are on an equal footing from the viewpoint of *wyrd* (=fate) and god as the distributor of strength. In the words of Beowulf we can know how the author regarded these warriors. The text runs as follows:

> Nelle ic beorges weard
> oferfléon fōtes trem, ac unc [furður] sceal
> weorðan æt wealle, swā unc wyrd getēoð,
> Metod manna gehwæs.
>
> (ll. 2524-27)

Beowulf calls both the dragon and himself not in the plural form but in the dual: *unc*. In l. 2526 he says "swa unc geteoð" (=as fate assigns us two) and in the next line as a variation he says: "Metod manna gehwæs" (=as the Measurer does to each man). Both Beowulf and the dragon are regarded as the "warriors" on the same level. It is interesting that Beowulf has come to be called king: *frōd folces weard* (= an old and wise guardian of the folk). The dragon's function is also "the guardian of the treasure" and is *frōd* (= old and wise). The adjective, *frōd*, belongs to both the warriors. On this point John D. Niles provides an interesting comment:

> The terms by which the poet refers to him never express moral condemnation, but rather imply respect for his function of guardianship. He is the "protector" of the hoard, the "shepherd of treasures" (*frætwa hyrde*), much as an

earthly king is the "shepherd of the tribe" (*folces hyrde*).[13]

It is interesting that in Nile's opinion the poet regards the dragon's function as a respectable one. The dragon is not only a destroyer but also has some other aspect in himself. The monster is something different from a human being, but the *Beowulf*-poet never treats the fight as something supernatural or miraculous. This is the essential part of the dragon fight.

The characteristics of the dragon in *Beowulf* are to be summarized as follows: 1) the dragon is eventually hostile to human beings; 2) he is guardian of a hoard; 3) he lives in a barrow; 4) he is very old; 5) he flies; 6) he vomits fire to burn the human habitation.[14]

As to the characteristic of the part 1), the text runs as follows:

                      Hordwynne fond
eald ūhtsceaða        opene standan,
sē ðe byrnende       biorgas sēceð,
nacod nīðdraca,      nihtes flēogeð
fȳre befangen;        hyne foldbūend
(swīðe ondrǣ) da(ð).  Hē gesēcean sceall
(ho)r(d on) hrūsan,   þǣr hē hǣðen gold
warað wintrum frōd;  ne byð him wihte ðȳ sēl.
      Swā se ðēodsceaða  þrēo hund wintra
hēold on hrūsan     hordærna sum

ēacencræftig,          oð ðæt hyne ān ābealch
mon on mōde;

(ll. 2270-81)

This passage explains all the characters of the dragon. Later we will examine them in detail. There is another noticeable passage:

Ne hēdde hē þæs heafolan,   ac sīo hand gebarn
mōdiges mannes,             þǣr hē his mǣges healp,
þæt hē þone nīðgæst         nioðor hwēne slōh,
secg on searwum,            þæt ðæt sweord gedēaf
fāh ond fǣted,              þæt ðæt fȳr ongon
sweðrian syððan.

(ll. 2697-2702)

The dragon is, in l. 2271, *ūhtsceaða* (depredator at twilight). He is old and finds the treasure standing open. He seeks a barrow; flies by night; the smooth hostile dragon burns and is wrapped in fire. People of the land are afraid of him. He had occupied his hoard for 300 years, until he was enraged in heart at the theft. In l. 2278 he is *ðeodsceaða* (people's foe); and in l. 2699 we find *nīðgæst* (malicious foe). These words represent the dragon's hostility.

2) He is guardian of a hoard. The text runs as follows:

|  | Sceolde lǣndaga |
| --- | --- |
| æþelinga ǣrgōd | ende gebīdan, |
| worulde līfes, | ond se wyrm somod, |
| þēah ðe hordwelan | hēolde lange. |

(ll. 2341-44)

|  | Hordweard onbād |
| --- | --- |
| earfoðlīce, | oð ðæt ǣfen cwōm; |

(ll. 2302-3)

In l. 2344, the poet says, "though he held the hoard wealth long," and in l. 2302 the dragon is called *hordweard* (=hoard guard). Indeed, the dragon has guarded his hoard for 300 years (l. 2278).

3) The dragon lives in a barrow.

|  | oð ðæt ān ongan |
| --- | --- |
| deorcum nihtum | draca rīcs[i]an, |
| sē ðe on hēa(ụm) h(ǣþ)e | hord beweotode, |
| stānbeorh stēapne; | stīg under læg |
| eldum uncūð. |  |

(ll. 2210-14)

|  | Hordwynne fond |
| --- | --- |
| eald ūhtsceaða | opene standan, |
| sē ðe byrnende | biorgas sēceð, |
| nacod nīðdraca, | nihtes flēogeð |

fȳre befangen;

(ll. 2270-74)

The dragon seeks *stānbeorh stēapne* (=high tone barrow, l. 2213) and seeks out *biorgas* (=barrows, l. 2272).
4) The dragon is an old demon.

|  | Weard unhīore, |
| gearo gūðfreca | goldmāðmas hēold |
| eald under eorðan; | |

(ll. 2413-15)

He has held gold under the earth since the old time.
5) He blows fire.

|  | wæs þære burnan wælm |
| heaðofȳrum hāt, | ne meahte horde nēah |
| unbyrnende | ǣnige hwīle |
| dēop gedȳgan | for dracan lēge. |

(ll. 2546-49)

In the duel between Beowulf and the dragon, the poet mentions a surging stream of hot battle-fire (l. 2547); nobody could endure the heat of the dragon's fire (l. 2549). The dragon wants to revenge himself for the theft of his precious cup with his fire. It is the dragon's most powerful weapon. These passages seem to reveal the identity of the monster:

"The dragon is the archenemy"[15] in the *Beowulf* epic. Two old warriors have their final duel and both of them die. The course of their battle is that of a fairy tale. Niles comments as follows:

> The poet tells of no entry to an uncanny realm, no divine aid, no miracle of a melting sword-blade or of light shining like the sun in the midst of darkness, no miraculous cleansing of the waters — in short, none of the wondrous details that make the combat with Grendel's mother one of the most astonishing adventures in English fiction. One fearsome combatant meets another, and that is all.[16]

The biggest difference between the Grendel episode and that of the dragon is that there is not any supernatural element in the dragon fight. It is a kind of paradox. Grendel and his mother are more humanized beings than the dragon. Grendel's mother takes revenge for her dead son. And before the duel Beowulf makes a boast against Grendel: he takes an oath that he will never wield any weapon, because Grendel does not have a sword. This is the typical ancient Germanic law of fairness. In the Grendel episode there are a number of mysterious elements but in the dragon fight there is nothing supernatural except the fact Beowulf's antagonist is a dragon.

## III

We have investigated the characteristics of the dragon in *Beowulf*. The dragon is exactly an imaginative being but he is close to a human being. From this point of view, we can set forth a hypothesis: the dragon may symbolize a certain kind of man. The demon's vengeful and disputable nature seems to remind us of the legend of Wieland in Germanic mythology.

In Germanic legends swords are often related to snakes. In the case of Hrunting, it is connected with the poetic images of weaving rings (l. 1667, *brogden-mæl*), with snakespattern (l. 1698, *wyrm-fāh*), and poison twigs (l. 1459, *ātertānum*). *Hring-boga* (=coiled creature, l. 2561) is one of the epithet of the dragon. Howell D. Chickering, Jr. says:

> Unferth's sword Hrunting is described by this last phrase, which derives from several associations: (a) the sword as a deadly serpent in battle; (b) the use of acid (poison) in manufacturing swords; (c) the agency of Woden, god of war, in watching over the smithy.[17]

It is noted that swords are connected with the serpent, poison, and the god of war that is the tutelary deity of the blacksmith, as well.

Serpents have some supernatural power in the mythology. In Greek mythology, ouroboros is a snake, and a river. When Achilles was a new born baby, he was dipped into the River Acheron by his mother. Then all his body except his heel became invulnerable to any weapon. In *Niebelungen Lied*, Sigfried takes a bath in a dragon's blood, then he is made invulnerable except at a point on his left shoulder. And in Old Norse tradition, the hero, Sigrðr, thrusts his sword into the belly of the dragon, Fafnir, like Wiglaf in *Beowulf*. The moment Sigrðr tastes the dragon's blood, he comes to understand birds' language. Thor and Miðgarðsormr, in Old Norse mythology, are ruined in Ragnarök. He is not only the god of lightning and thunder but also a god that has the function of a blacksmith.

The mythical blacksmith, Wieland, is lamed by a king to make him unable to run away from his court. When he finally gets away, he obtains wings to run away. At the same time, Wieland reveals his extraordinary strong vengeful intention.[18] His vengeful character is similar to that of the dragon in *Beowulf*. The dragon must be a symbol of a certain group of men who had knowledge of subterranean property. It is probable that the word, *wyrm* (=worm), symbolizes Wieland's lamed legs.

The Tubal-Cain figure embodies the forces of destruction.[19] In *Beowulf* the treasure guarded by the dragon is regarded as the work of giants:

> Đā ic on hlǣwe gefrægn        hord rēafian,
> eald enta geweorc              ānne mannan,
>
> (ll. 2773-74)

Giants in this context must be a people who is lost. For the ancient these strangers were Little People (=fairy) or the Giants. David Williams comments as follows:

> Every culture attributes mythical and magical properties to ore and gems besides adorning the invention of such elements and their exploitation with legends. Most cultures, as well, associate the dragon with these subterranean properties. The Christian legends, some of which we have seen already, attributed the mining of metals and gems from the earth to the depravity of demons who instructed early man in the magic needed to use these elements.[20]

The technology of the blacksmith has been connected with the god of war and magic. Fire is demonic but the blacksmith utilizes fire at will.

The sword and the Tubal-Cain figure could be connected with the dragon.[21] Here we should like to see the etymological aspects of the dragon:

> Der Drache dagegen werde nicht als Höllengeist, sondern als fremdartiges Wesen aufgefaßt, und deshalb bedeute *gæst*, wenn von ihm gebraucht, 'Gast'. Klaeber, der Angl. 35,251

geneigt war, Holthausen recht zu geben, folgt in seiner Ausgabe vielmehr Chambers. Tatsache ist jedenfalls, daß der Drache nie *gāst*, wohl aber *gryregiest* 'grausiger Gast' (2560) genannt wird. Der *nicor*, das Wasserungetüm, das Beowulf erlegt, wird ebenfalls als *gryrelīc gist* 'grausiger Gast' bezeichnet (1441). Idg. *\*ghostis*=lat. *hostis*, urgerm. *\*ʒastiz*, ae. *giest, gist, gest, gæst* bedeutete ursprünglich 'Fremdling', woraus sich im Lateinischen die Bedeutung 'Feind', in Germanischen 'Gast' entwickelte. Doch hat das Wort im Altgermanischen neben dem Begriff 'hospes' noch etwas von dem Grundbegriff 'Fremdling' bewahrt; so in *gryrelīc gist*.[22]

The dragon is regarded not as a devil in hell but as a strange being, and therefore it is rendered *gæst*, whenever the word is given as "guest". Klaeber who, in Angl. 35 p. 251, was inclined to mean "guest", even in his edition he followed Chambers, and Holthausen admitted that is was right. Anyhow it is a fact that the dragon is never just a guest, but will be *gryregiest* "terrible guest" (2560). The *nicor*, the water-monster, which Beowulf kills, is also characterized as *gryrelic gist* "terrible guest" (1441). Idg. *\*ghostis*=Latin *hostis*, proto-Germanic *\*ʒastiz*, O.E. *giest, gist, gest, gæst* originally signifies "stranger", from which developed in Latin "enemy" and in Old Germanics "guest". But the word in Old Germanic has kept the idea "*hospes* (guest)" as well, but the original idea is "stranger", as in *gryrelīc gist*.

From the etymological point of view, the dragon is

represented as a "terrible guest" or a "stranger". The dragon is, originally, something that came from somewhere unknown. Hilda Ellis Davidson considers that the dragon is from the East.[23] A.M. Arent regards the Germanic dragon image as Roman in origin. She comments as follows:

> Pictorial representation of the serpent-dragon motif in the Germanic north may have received added stimulus from Roman coins and from the flags of Roman legions which portrayed the "draco". But such a universal symbol no doubt overlapped with indigenous conceptions, for in Germanic literature the Romance *draco* gradually replaced the Germanic *ormr*, *wurm*, *lindwurm* (Icel. *dreki*, OHG. *dracho*) in the whole gamut of its connotations.[24]

It is probable that a part of the image of the dragon is from the Roman Army. In the other part of her article, Arent says that "the Roman legions let their dragon banners fly".[25] It is probable that the more advanced Roman weapons were introduced into the Germanics. We know that: "The borderline between myth and history is a fluid one."[26] It is highly probable that there must have been a confusion between the dragon image and the strong army.

The dragon image has many elements in itself. It must symbolize the men who had certain subterranean knowledge and certain martial arts. That caused the imaginative horror, and then it was crystallized into the dragon image.

## Conclusion

It is a fact that the dragon is a product of human imagination. The dragon in *Beowulf* is not only a monster in a fairy-tale, but has some other noticeable elements. Arent says that "The dragon is the epitome of all dreadful foes."[27] Human imagination often visualizes some kind of enemies as destructive monsters.[28] Strangers, as well, often stimulate human imagination, especially when they are invaders. They are often described as dreadful monsters.

The dragon is a demon, though he is given many humanized elements in *Beowulf*. The way the monster is described is more like a human being than a monster. In the Germanic legend, Wieland, the mythical blacksmith, has vengeful spite against his enemies who have lamed him. And his art as a blacksmith must have been demonic for the ancient Germanic people. The dragon and the blacksmith have common elements: fire; sword; subterranean precious metals; lame like a serpent; demonic; vengeance. The dragon in *Beowulf* is not a monster but symbolizes men who have knowledge as blacksmiths and the martial art of fire. He is the richest creation of the ancient human civilization.

## Notes

1. M.S. Cotton Tibelius. B.i., Maxims II, 26-27. Elliott Van Kirk Dobbie (ed.): *The Anglo-Saxon Minor Poems* The Anglo-Saxon Poetic Records VI (New York: Columbia University Press, 1942), p.56.
2. David Williams, *Cain and Beowulf: A Study in Secular Allegory*. (Toronto: University of Toronto Press, 1982), p.37.
3. Williams, ibid., p.61.
4. Alan K. Brown, "The Firedrake in *Beowulf*". *Neophilologus*, 64 (1980), p.443.
5. Brown, ibid., p.450.
6. Hilda Ellis Davidson, "The Hills of the Dragon: Anglo-Saxon Burial Mounds in Literature and Archaeology", *Folk-lore*, 61 (1950), p.181.
7. Davidson, ibid., p.179.
8. Williams, ibid., p.63.
9. J.R.R. Tolkien, "*Beowulf*: The Monsters and the Critics", in *Anthology of Beowulf Criticism* ed. Lewis E. Nicholson (Notre Dame, Indiana: University of Notre Dame Press, 1989), p.66.
10. Edward B. Irving Jr., *Rereading Beowulf* (Philadelphia: University of Pennsylvania Press, 1989), p.101.
11. Irving Jr., ibid., p.101.
12. Frederick Klaeber, ed. *Beowulf and the Fight at Finnsburg*. (Lexington: D. C. Heath, 1950). All quotations henceforth are from this edition.
13. John D. Niles, *Beowulf: The Poem and Its Tradition*. (Cambridge MA: Harvard University Press, 1983), pp.24-25.
14. On further detail, see E.B. Irving Jr., Ibid., p.31.
15. A Margaret Arent, "The Heroic Pattern: Old Germanic Helmets, *Beowulf* and *Grettis saga*", in *Old Norse Literature and Mythology: A Symposium*. ed. Edgar C. Polomé. (Austin; University of Texas, 1969), p.153.

16. Niles, ibid., p.28.
17. Howell D. Chickering Jr., *Beowulf, A Dual-Language Edition*. (New York: Doubleday, 1977), p.343.
18. Teiji Yoshimura, *Geruman-Shinwa*. (Tokyo: Yomiuri-Shinbunsha, 1972), pp.35-36.
19. Williams, ibid., p.61.
20. Williams, ibid., p.60.
21. Martin Puhvel, *Beowulf and Celtic Tradition*. (Ontario: Wilfred Laurier University Press), p.30.
22. Johannes Hoops, *Kommentar zum Beowulf*. (Heidelberg: Carl Winter, 1965), pp.29-30.
23. Davidson, ibid., p.182.
24. Arent, ibid., pp.141-2.
25. Arent, ibid., p.151.
26. Arent, ibid., p.141.
27. Arent, ibid., p.152.
28. Arent, ibid., p.141.

# The 'Thryth-Offa Digression' in *Beowulf*

Norman E. Eliason sets out to prove in his article, "The 'Thryth-Offa Digression' in *Beowulf*"[1] that the two genealogies of the Angles and the Geats could be united by the Geatish queen, Hygd. He asserts that the fusion of the two genealogies is intentional.[2] The passage, Eliason says, from l. 1925 to l. 1962 speaks not of two women but of one, Hygd, throughout.[3]

He insists: "before her marriage to Hygelac she had been the wife of Offa and had born him a son who was the ancestor of the royal line of Mercia, it all fits together quite well."[4] His idea is quite interesting but not quite acceptable.

The so-called Modþryð episode begins from l. 1931. Hygelac is introduced a few lines before, in l. 1923ff, after Beowulf's arrival to Geatland. And in his stronghold he lives with his youthful, wise and accomplished queen, Hygd. The poet praises her as an ideal queen of the Germanic tradition.[5] The comment (ll. 1927b-29a) that she had dwelt a few winters in the wall of the stronghold can be understood because she was very young. After a sudden stop to the very short account of Hygd, and without any explanation, the poet begins to tell of an apparently different woman, Modþryð, the queen of Offa. It seems that the poet introduced her in order to enhance the impression of Hygd.[6] She is mentioned "*swiðe geong* (very young)" in l. 1926a. Then the queen Modþryð appears as a counterpart of Hygd. The young, haughty, violent, cruel, tyrannical Modþryð cruelly murdered any man, except her father, who dared to look on her in the daylight or who displeased her. However Hemming's kinsman, the king Offa of Angle, put a stop to her crimes.[7] She was sent of Offa's court. After her marriage to him, she forms a parallel as far as her character is concerned. She had a son, Ēomer, the ancestor of the Mercian royal family.[9] In short, the young, tyrannical Modþryð forms a strong contrast to the young, very much loved and generous Hygd of the maiden action.

Eliason offers one reason for the sudden shift of l. 1931ff. This is the starting point of Eliason's assumption. It is as follows:

> There is another solution, and though modern scholars rarely if ever even mention it, it deserves reconsideration. Up to about a hundred years ago, the passage was commonly construed as referring to a single queen. I think there is something to be said in its favor. Accordingly, I propose to reexamine the objections to it and to see if the passage can not legitimately be read thus.[10]

And Eliason introduces the view of C.W.M. Grein's famous essay.[11] This is the opposite of his assumption. He introduces it as follows:

> With the publication of Grein's famous essay in 1862, the presence of both Hygd and "Thryth" in the passage was firmly established, together with the reasons for thinking this must be so. In ridding the passage of most of the fantastic explanations that it had had, Grein performed a notable service, and the lucidity of his explanation lent weight to the reasons he gave. These were very simple. Offa, he maintained, lived in the mid-fourth century and Hygelac at the beginning of the sixth, and therefore Hygd could not possibly have been the wife of both. Her name too argued against it, for Offa's wife was named "Thryth" or something like it, a fact which he claimed was supported by the St. Albans account. Of these reasons of Grein's, the first (Offa's date) was and remains by all odds the more important, the second (his wife's name) being more or less incidental. Neither seems ever to have been effectively challenged. In current scholarship both are accepted without serious question or essential modification.[12]

As a matter of historical fact, the wife of Offa II, king of Mercia, was named Cynethryth, as is so inscribed on coins.[13]

Eliason declares that in these 37 lines (ll. 1925-62) the poet's feat is hidden.[14] His assumption is as follows: a wicked girl, first called Modþryð, married Offa and had a son; after

Offa's early death, she went to Geatland, then married Hygelac again; in the Geatish court she was called Hygd.

To prove his assumption, he offers two pieces of evidence: 1) the transition from Hygd to Modþryð is no more abrupt than many other transitions; 2) Offa and Hygelac are almost contemporaries.

However the key to this problem is the date of Offa's lifetime. Eliason admits as follows:

> Thus the crux of the whole matter is the date of Offa's life. If he antedated Hygd by a century or more —— as Grein insisted and as has been confidently reiterated ever since —— it is impossible that she could have been his wife. If the evidence bears this out, my reading of the passage is wrong.[15]

Now here are my objections to Eliason's assumption: 1) The transition (l. 1931b) is sudden enough, like many other transitions. And an abrupt change from one person to another is not unknown in *Beowulf*. It is a typical device of the *Beowulf*-poet; 2) l. 1931b ff. Modþryð ō wæg... is the only possible reading that makes sense with reference to the following context; 3) the genealogy of the Mercian royal line, according to ll. 1944-62, does not fit Eliason's genealogy.

1) An abrupt change from one person to another, as in l. 1931, is not unknown in *Beowulf*. It is characteristic of the poet's technique. And the transition of l. 1931 is sudden enough, because in the same line, the former sentence speaks

of Hygd and the latter speaks of an altogether different woman, Modþryð. This is abrupt enough, like many other transitions. A. Bonjour indicates that the introduction of an episode in a sudden change is the poet's favorite device.[16] And another *Beowulf* scholar, H. D. Chickering, Jr. asserts, "He is better when com-posing, putting disparate things together, than when he takes a long panoramic view down across the years."[17]

2) This is a view opposite to Eliason's note 6. In lines 1931b ff. "Modþryð ō wæg" is the only possible reading that makes sense with reference to the following context and fits the habits of those days. In l. 1931b it is writtern Modþryðo but Modþryð must be the name of a woman. And Modþryð with the following ō is a absolutely impossible for that time. It is the third syllable. That cannot have, after a long syllable, *ō*. So *ō* must be a word of its own. Modþryð is the feminine proper name of the lady. And *ō* is the emphatically stressed form of *ā*, the usual *ā*, long *a*, with the meaning of "always." The long *a* in Anglo-Saxon words that are stressed very often in context changes to *ō*. *A* changes to *ō*. And this is represented then by the scribes by *ō*.[18]

Hoops gives the translation of this line. His translation is as follows: "M übte (immer), die hochfahrende Volkskönigin, schlecklichen Frevel," (=Modþryð had (always) practiced, the haughty queen of people, terrible crimes).[19] This deviates far from Eliason's translation in his note.[20]

3) Eliason mentions that the problem is Offa's lifetime.[21]

If it is proved that Offa's lifetime is earlier than Hygelac's, it must be said that Eliason's assumption is unacceptable. The genealogy of the Mercian royal line, according to ll. 1944-62, is as follows:

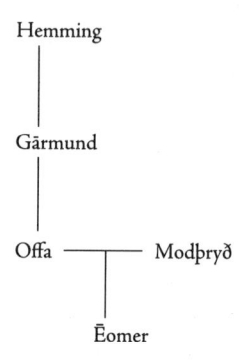

```
         Hemming
            |
         Gārmund
            |
         Offa ——————— Modþryð
                |
             Ēomer
```

The first two names are mythical and the other names are historical.

Now let me introduce the outline of the Indo-European myth. The pagan religion of the Anglo-Saxons is fundamentally identical with that of other Germanic peoples. The common Germanic religion is deeply rooted in the religious concept of all ancient Indo-European peoples.

The first primary being (Urwesen) is thought to be either a gigantic egg or an androgeneous giant. These two chief forms of primary being are connected with the origin of the world in the Indo-European concept. According to the egg-myth, the upper half of the world became heaven and its lower half the earth. According to the giant myth, the world was formed by the self-sacrifice of the giant: his flesh became the earth, his skull heaven, his blood the ocean, his brain clouds and so on. According to another version of the giant myth, the father heaven and the mother earth were formed in its left arm-pit. According to the giant myth, the world had the form of a house. The giant as the primary architect supported heaven by means of a gigantic column as a roof above the earth.

The father heaven is the fertilizer of the mother earth. And the mother earth is the giver of field goods. But the fertilizer of both is given by the primary being. The father heaven and the mother earth have four sons in holy marriage. The *first son* is the god of heaven and light, furthermore the god of law, order, war and the protector of the clans. The *second son* is the god of earth and the god of water and the sacrificial fire. The second son has a twin brother. He is thought to fight against monsters and demons. He is the god of thunderstorms. The *third son* is the god of the atmosphere and as such the god of winds and storms and the leader of the dead souls which are carried off by storms or winds. He is accompanied by a band of killing women.

The god of earth and the god of heaven beget with the mother earth (their mother) a son each, who are regarded as twin brothers. They are youthful brotherly gods. They are healers and helpers in need, particularly in battle and in distress at sea. They are also helpers at birth. They are connected with horses and considered as morning and evening star. The god of earth begets with his mother also a daughter. She becomes the wife of the third son.

Among the Indo-European family of gods, the ancestor of the family is the most important.

The Germanic/Anglo-Saxon family of gods shows the same genealogical structure. The family-tree of the Anglo-Saxon gods with Old English names is as follows:

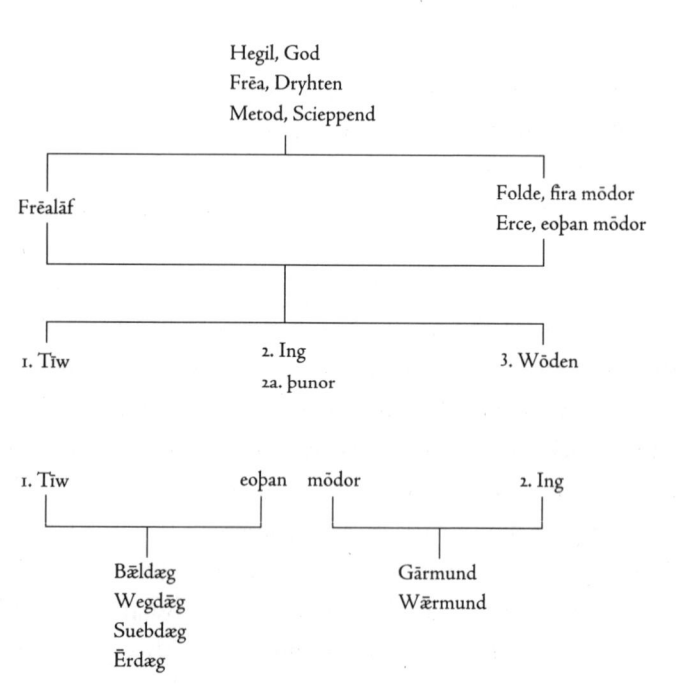

```
                    Hegil, God
                    Frēa, Dryhten
                    Metod, Scieppend
                         |
    ┌────────────────────┴────────────────────┐
                                      Folde, fira mōdor
Frēalāf                               Erce, eoþan mōdor
    └────────────────────┬────────────────────┘
                         |
    ┌────────────────────┼────────────────────┐
  1. Tīw            2. Ing                 3. Wōden
                    2a. þunor
```

```
  1. Tīw        eoþan  mōdor          2. Ing
    └─────────────┘     └───────────────┘
           |                    |
       Bældæg               Gārmund
       Wegdæg               Wǣrmund
       Suebdæg
       Ērdæg
```

All these gods have the same features and functions as the corresponding Indo-European divinities. It is to be noted that the primary god and the youthful brotherly gods have a variety of names each pointing to a special feature or function.[22]

Now we turn to the Mercian royal pedigree again. Hemming and Gārmund are the mythical part of the genealogy. The historical genealogy begins from the name of Offa. Hemming is the god Ing. In other words, Hemming is, from an etymological point of view, the begetter of bodies, hama (=covering). Ing is the begetter, father. Hemming is the begetter of hama, of something belonging to a body, that is to say, the begetter of human beings. And the hamija changes by West-Germanic doubling of the consonant before *j* and by umlaut to Hemming: begetter of bodies.[23] Gārmund is the youthful brotherly god, connected with a horse.[24] Ēomer means etymologically "famous horse."[25] The grandson is called after features connected with his grandfather, Gārmund.

The genealogy of the Mercian royal line according to the *Anglo-Saxon Chronicle*, age 626 (Penda genealogy).[26] It contains two mistakes. Two names, Wihtlæg and Angelþeow, do not link the genealogy. They are mere appositions to a following and a preceding name.[27] If these mistakes are eliminated one arrives at the following genealogy:

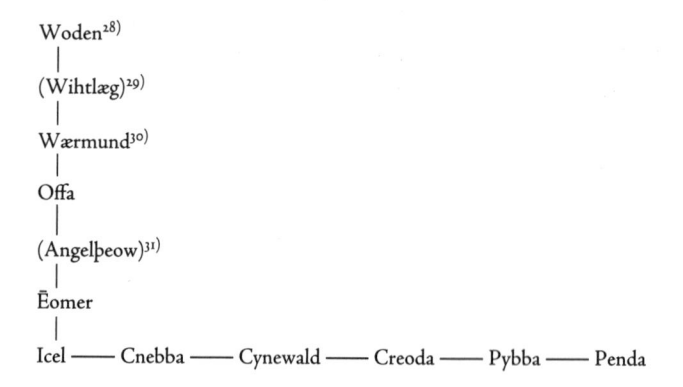

```
Woden[28)
  |
(Wihtlæg)[29)
  |
Wærmund[30)
  |
Offa
  |
(Angelþeow)[31)
  |
Ēomer
  |
Icel ——— Cnebba ——— Cynewald ——— Creoda ——— Pybba ——— Penda
```

If one starts from the year 626 (Penda genealogy) and attributes to each link a time span of 30 years, one arrives for Offa of the Angles at the year 416A.D. ($626 - 7 \times 30 = 416$).[32] This date does not agree with Eliason's assumption that Offa and Hygelac were almost contemporaries and Grein's assumption that Offa lived in the mid-fourth century.

Offa's accession to the throne occurred about 416A.D. So his death-date becomes, presumably, 446A.D. The date of Hygelac's death is well known. He died in 520 or 521A.D. at the time of the raid on Frisia. It is reported by a historian and chronicler, St. Gregory of Tours (ca. 540-594 A.D.), who dates the last and fatal raid against Frisians, for certain, 520 or 521 A.D.[33] There lay about 74 years ($520 - 446 = 74$) between the death date of Offa and Hygelac. If Hygelac was still young when he died, they could not be contemporaries.[34]

In Klaeber's assumption, the return of Beowulf to

Hygelac's hall occurred in 515 A.D.[35] And in Eliason's assumption, Hygd's marriage to Hygelac took place in 510 A.D.,[36] since Hygd had dwelt only few winters in Hygelac's stronghold. If Hygelac married Offa's widow, she could not have been swiðe geong (very young), because she had to wait 64 years (510 - 446=64) after Offa's death. Here it is proved that Eliason's assumption is not true. And Hygd was not Offa's queen, Modþryð.

---

## Notes

1) Norman E. Eliason, "The 'Thryth-Offa' Digression in *Beowulf*," *Medieval and Linguistic Studies in Honor of Francis Peabody Magoun, Jr.*, ed, Jess B. Bessinger, Jr., and Robert P. Creed (New York: New York University Press, 1965), pp. 124-38.
2) Eliason, p. 131.
3) Eliason, p. 126.
4) Eliason, p. 127.
5) Cf. H.D. Chickering, Jr., *Beowulf, A Dual-Language Edition* (New York: Doubleday, 1977), pp. 349-52.
6) John. R. Clark Hall., *Beowulf and the Finnesburg Fragment, a Translation into Modern English Prose*. A new edition completely revised with notes and an introduction by C. L. Wrenn, with prefatory remarks by J.R.R. Tolkien (London: George Allen & Unwin, 1980), p. 118.
7) Johannes Hoops, *Kommentar zum Beowulf* (1932; rpt. Heidelberg: Carl Winter, 1965), p.215.
8) Furthermore, Modþryð's change from bad to good forms a contrast to Heremod's change from good to bad, from a young, famous paragon

of a hero to a blood thirsty, cruel tyrant (cf. l. 901 ff., l. 1709 ff.); cf. Adrien Bonjour, *The Digressions in Beowulf* (Oxford: Blackwell, 1970), p.55.

9) The poet praises Offa, his father (Gārmund) and his son (Ēomer). It seems to praise not only Offa but his whole royal line. The audience of Mercia or any Anglian territory connected with Mercia would have been interested in the glorious ancestor of Mercia. Cf. Eliason p.126; R. W. Chambers, *Beowulf: An Introduction to the Study of the Poem*, 3rd edition with a supplement by C. L. Wrenn (1959: rpt. Cambridge University Press, 1972), p.540.

10) Eliason p.125.

11) C.M.W. Grein, "Die historischen Verhältnisse des Beowulfliedes," *Jahrbuch für romanische und englische Literatur*, IV (1862), 260-85; cf. Eliason pp.135-36, note 15.

12) Eliason, p.128.

13) Eliason, p.129; cf. Chambers, p.37.

14) Eliason, p.132.

15) Eliason, p.129.

16) Bonjour, p.54; For example, the introduction of Heremod's episodes is rather sudden. And the introduction of some other episodes, too, seems to be rather abrupt, especially after l. 2200. Cf. l. 2200 ff., l. 2354 ff., l. 2397 ff., l. 2425 ff., l. 2611 ff., l. 2922 ff..

17) Chickering, Jr., p.355.

18) Schneider, ibid., p.65; cf. Hoops, p.212; Elliot van Kirk Dobbie, *Beowulf and Judith*. The Anglo-Saxon Poetic Records, IV (New York and London: Columbia University Press, 1953), pp.214-15.

19) Hoops, ibid., p.212.

20) Eliason, p.134; Schneider, ibid. p.60.

21) Eliason, p.129.

22) Schneider, ibid., pp.199-204; cf. Schneider, *Die germanischen Runennamen* (Meisenheim: Anton Hain K. G., 1956), p.357.

23) Schneider, ibid. p. 71.
24) Schneider, *Die germ. Runennamen*, pp.378-87.
25) Frederick Klaeber, *Beowulf and the Fight at Finnsburg*, edited with introduction, bibliography, notes, glossary, and appendices. 3rd edition with first and second supplements (Lexington: D. C. Heath, 1950), p.434.
26) Charles Plummer and John Earle, *Two of the Saxon Chronicles Parallel* (Oxford: Oxford University Press, 1929), pp.24-25.
27) In the genealogical links, certain names or certain members have at times two names. They are either called A or B. Then, later, a genealogist thought that the apposition was an additional link in the genealogy. And then a lot of mistakes occur. Cf. Schneider, ibid. p. 19.
28) The original ancestor was not Woden but Ing. He is the father of Wærmund. Letter received from Prof. Schneider, 26 November, 1981; Ing was dismissed by the tribe who believed in Woden. Cf. Watanabe Shoichi, "Hengist to Horsa nitsuite," *Eibungaku To Eigogaku*, No.3 (1966), pp.116-32.
29) Wihtlæg is an apposition to Wærmund. Letter received from Prof. Schneider, 26 November, 1981.
30) Wærmund is an apposition to Gārmund.
31) Angelþeow is "servant of the Angles." Angelþeow is an apposition to Offa. Schneider, ibid. p.73.
32) Hoops, p.210.
33) Clark Hall, p. 10; Klaeber, pp. xxxviii-xxxix.
34) If Klaeber's assumption of Hygelac's lifetime (A. D. 475-521) on p.xxxviii is precise, it will be impossible, of course, for him to be contemporary with Offa.
35) Klaeber, p.xxxix.
36) Eliason, p.129.

# A Historical Survey of *Beowulf* Studies
— From the 19th to the 20th century —

The extant text of *Beowulf* is contained in a codex called Vitellius A XV of the Cotton Library. From the viewpoint of paleography, the *Beowulf* text was written around 1000 A.D. by two scribes: the hand of scribe A wrote down lines 1-1939a and the hand of scribe B the rest of the manuscript. After the Protestant Reformation by Henry VIII in 1535-39, the manuscript survived and was acquired by "a learned antiquarian", Laurence Nowell, who is also known to have written his name and date, 1563, on the top of the first page of the text.[1] Nowell's books are now called "Nowell Codex". After the death of Nowell in 1576, his books came into the collection of Sir Robert Cotton (1571-1631).

In 1705, Humfrey Wanley, who is called "the first great scholar of Anglo-Saxon manuscripts," introduced the story of *Beowulf* into his catalogue of the surviving manuscripts. In 1805, Sharon Turner published the first text of *Beowulf* in his history of *Beowulf* research. It includes citations and inaccurate translations of *Beowulf*.[2] He continued publishing the enlarged editions one after another.[3]

In 1786 Grimmur Jonsson Thorkelin, a Danish scholar

who was an Icelander by birth, hired a professional copyist to transcribe the poem, and after studying the transcript, he recopied it. After the Copenhagen fire of 1807, Thorkelin resumed the task to publish an edition and Latin translation of *Beowulf* in 1815. Now it is known that Thorkelin's text and translation has little value. George Clark completes the history of the *Beowulf* study from the viewpoint of paleography:

> Wanley's catalog, Thorkelin's transcript (lent to various others and indeed recopied), Turner's excerpts, and Thorkelin's edition and translation brought *Beowulf* into the center of Anglo-Saxon studies where the poem remains to the present day. ... At the end of the eighteenth and the beginning of the nineteenth centuries, *Beowulf* challenged antiquarians, philologists, and scholars to unravel its literal sense, fathom its artistic design, discover its place in literary history, and assess its merit as a work of art.[4]

Nowadays, the texts and translations of the eighteenth and early nineteenth centuries are regarded to be of little value. However we should know and appreciate the fact that we are dependent on the endeavour of the scholars in the former centuries. Finally we have a facsimile of the manuscript published by the Early English Text Society in 1882. It is a transliteration of the text by a German scholar, Zupitza, and a photographical facsimile with transcription and notes.[5]

Since the first *Beowulf*-text was published in the 19th century quite a number of scholars have been studying the poem both linguistically and as a literary work, and in literary criticism the theme of Christianity is often treated in various ways. From the 19th century on, it seems that scholars have treated *Beowulf* either from the viewpoint of Christianity or according to Greek examples. In 1855, Benjamin Thorpe commented on the production of *Beowulf* as follows:

> With respect to this the oldest heroic poem in any Germanic tongue, my opinion is, that it is not an original production of the Anglo-Saxon muse, but a metrical paraphrase of an heroic Saga composed in the south-west of Sweden, in the old common language of the North, and probably brought to this country during the sway of the Danish dynasty. It is in this light only that I can view a work evincing a knowledge of Northern localities and persons hardly to be acquired by a native of England in those days of ignorance with regard to remote foreign parts. And what interest could an Anglo-Saxon feel in the valorous feats of his deadly foes, the Northmen? in the encounter of a Sweo-Gothic hero with a monster in Denmark? or with a fire-drake in his own country? The answer, I think, is obvious —— *none whatever.*
>
> This hypothesis may, perhaps, serve to account for some at least of the deviations from the historic or, as our continental

brethren would prefer to regard them, mythic traditions contained in the early annals of England and the North, many of which may, no doubt, be placed to the account of the paraphrast. Let those to whom this view may appear rash, consult any Anglo-Saxon version of a Latin author, or even a metrical paraphrase of a prose writer in his own tongue, and, on seeing its numerous misconceptions of the original, he will, unless I greatly err, considerably qualify, if not change, his opinion. From the allusions to Christianity contained in the poem, I do not hesitate to regard it as a Christian paraphrase of a heathen Saga, and those allusions as interpolations of the paraphrast, whom I conceive to have been a native of England of Scandinavian parentage.[6]

In those days, scholars recognized the existence of the Christian allusions, but they did not regard them as forming the main theme of the epic. His comment reveals that *Beowulf*-scholarship was not well advanced but rather simple in his days. But in five decades from Thorpe's text, a German scholar, Richard Wülker, treats *Beowulf* in his voluminous work, *Geschichte der Englishchen Literatur*. He says as follows:

> Das Motiv im Beowulfliede ist dasselbe, das durch alle Heldendichtungen der germanischen Völker hindurchklingt: Ruhm ist das Beste, was der Mensch auf Erden erlangen kann. Ruhm aber wird erlangt durch furchtlose Tapferkeit.

A Historical Survey of *Beowulf* Studies

Beowulf kommt von ferne her, um Grendel zu erschlagen und sich dauernden Nachruhm zu erwerben im Gedächtnis der Menschen. Dem Fürsten aber, der tapfere Helden um sich versammeln will, ist es Pflicht, kühne Thaten reichlich zu belohnen; Freigebigkeit ist die Haupttugend des Herrschers. Damit jedoch der Führer Heldenthaten vollbringen könne, müssen ihm seine Mannen treu zur Seite stehen: daher wie für den Fürsten Freigebigkeit, so ist Treue gegen seinen Herrn das Hauptgebot für den Untergebenen. Nur durch die Treue der Mannen kann der Herr Macht und Ansehen erlangen. Solange sich die Geaten treu um Beowulf scharen, vollführt er seine Heldenthaten. Er fällt, als sie ihn treulos verlassen, wie auch Sigfrid im Nibelungenliede, der umbesiegbare Held, nur durch Untreue getötet werden kann.[7]

The motif in the epic, *Beowulf*, is the same thing, which is common though all the heroic epic of the Germanic people: fame is the best thing, which men on earth can achieve by all means. Fame will be barely got only through bold behaviour. Beowulf comes from afar to slaughter Grendel and to get eternal fame in the memory of the people. It is a duty for the lord to get brave warriors, to reward their brave deeds to the full; then the leader could accomplish brave deeds, and his followers must help him faithfully: therefore as generosity is essential to the lord, faith to his lord is the essential law for his followers. Only through the faith of the followers can the lord achieve might and fame. As long as the faithful Geats rally round Beowulf, he accomplishes his brave deeds. He falls in action, when they forsake him, as Siegfried, the unequaled hero, as well can be killed only through insincerity.

This is the typical concept of old Germanic literature in those days. It is interesting that he compares Beowulf with Siegfried. According to Wülker, they are killed only when they are betrayed by their followers, and he considers that Christianity is the later addition to the original epic.[8]

As to the interpretation of *Beowulf* in the 19th century, H.M. Chadwick summarizes it as follows:

> Until within the last few years the majority of scholars believed that *Beowulf* was a composite work. This theory was most fully developed in the writings of Müllenhoff and ten Brink. According to the former the poem was made up from four separate lays, though in its present form nearly half of it is the work of interpolators. The latter likewise traced the origin of the poem to lays, but explained its inconsistencies as being due not to extensive interpolations but to the combination of two parallel versions. In regard to the relative antiquity of the various parts of the poem there was great divergence of opinion both between these scholars and generally.[9]

There were a number of different interpretations of the poem, most of which sound rather immature today. *Beowulf*-scholars had to wait for the appearance of Schücking and Tolkien in the former half of the 20th century, before a truly noticeable opinion came out.

Before the orthodox interpretation of *Beowulf*, this work of art faced a fairly severe criticism in 1904:

> It is plain from Aristotle's words that the *Iliad* and the *Odyssey* were in this, as in all respects, above and beyond the other Greek epics known to Aristotle. Homer had not to wait for *Beowulf* to serve as a foil to his excellence. That was provided in the other epic poems of Greece, in the cycle of Troy, in the epic stories of Theseus and Haracles.[10]

It seems that Ker considered Homer's *Odyssey* to be much above *Beowulf*.

The epic, *Beowulf*, has been considered as a Christian poem since Frederick Klaeber's "Die christlichen Elemente im *Beowulf*" in 1911 and 1912. This article seems to have fixed the Christian interpretation of the epic.

In spite of the assertions of F.A. Blackburn and H.M. Chadwick at the end of nineteenth century and the beginning of the twentieth century, the interpretation of *Beowulf* as a pagan work of art became rather out of vogue. One of the main causes of the dominance of Christian interpretation seems to be the publication of Frederick

Klaeber's text of *Beowulf*. In his works he emphasizes that the language and thoughts are essentially Christian. In his edition he comments as follows:

> Predominantly Christian are the general tone of the poem and its ethical viewpoint. We are no longer in a genuine pagan atmosphere. The sentiment has been softened and purified. The virtues of moderation, unselfishness, consideration for others are practised and appreciated. The manifest readiness to express gratitude to God on all imaginable occasions (625 ff., 1397 f., 928 f., 1778 f., 1626 f., 1997 f., 2794 ff., 227 f.), and the poet's sympathy with weak and unfortunate beings like Scyld the foundling (7, 46) and even Grendel (e.g. 105, 721, 973, 975, 1351) and his mother (1546 f.), are typical of the new note. Particularly striking is the moral refinement of the two principal characters, Bēowulf and Hrōðgār. Those readers who, impressed by Bēowulf's martial appearance at the beginning of the action, expect to find an aggressive warrior hero of the Achilles or Sigfrit type, will be disposed at times to think him somewhat tame, sentimental, and fond of talking. Indeed, the final estimate of the hero's character by his own faithful thanes lamenting his death is chiefly a praise of Bēowulf's gentleness and kindness: *cwǣdon þæt hē wǣre wyruldcyning[a]/manna mildust ond monðwǣrust,/lēodum līðost ond lofgeornost* 3180.[11]

For Klaeber *Beowulf* cannot be but a Christian work. His idea sounds rather excessive, because the ideal concepts of the Christian and pagan ethics are partly identical and partly similar to each other. Yet, predominantly the epic is not a Christian work in itself.

Klaeber's study is widely accepted by scholars who believe that Christianity pervades the epic. Though his research is widely consented to, his studies are dependent on parallels with the Bible. Klaeber's *Beowulf*-text is the best of its kind, though his criticism is out of vogue.

Klaeber's faithful follower, Dorothy Whitelock, regards the author as a Christian poet "who was responsible for giving the poem the general shape and tone in which it has survived."[12] She considers that the audience could understand and was familiar with the descriptions from the Bible.[13] So it is likely, she remarks, that the audience could fully understand the Christian allusions or "Christian poetic phraseology" even if they are somewhat inexact.[14] Her idea is typically summarized in the following passage:

> But one can show that, if a heathen poem on this subject once existed, it must have been very different from the work that has come down to us. As has often been pointed out, the Christian element is not merely superimposed; it permeates the poem.[15]

She tries to understand the epic through the social and cultural background of the Anglo-Saxon after the Christian conversion. It may be possible that Whitelock's audience would have appreciated the work in Whitelock's own manner.

In 1936, J.R.R. Tolkien presented a magnificent lecture. His marvelous talk at the British Academy marks a turning point in the history of *Beowulf* criticism. Tolkien provides us with an interesting comment as follows:

> 'In structure', it was said of *Beowulf*, 'it is curiously weak, in a sense preposterous,' though great merits of detail were allowed. In structure actually it is curiously strong, in a sense inevitable, though there are defects of detail. The general design of the poet is not only defensible, it is, I think, admirable.[16]

Tolkien considers the epic as the whole in harmony. Also in the sense of structure, though there is some 'defects of detail'. The structure of the epic makes the epic unified. For the *Beowulf*-poet the epic is not a musical or artistic work but a narrative poem.[17] In a sense, the work cannot be categorized in modern terms. Tolkien again comments as follows:

> *Beowulf* is not an 'epic', not even a magnified 'lay'. No terms borrowed from Greek or other literatures exactly fit: there is no reason why they should. Though if we must have a term, we should choose rather 'elegy'. It is a heroic-elegiac poem; and in a sense all its first 3, 136 lines are the prelude to a dirge: *him þa gegiredan Geata leode ad ofer eorðan unwaclicne*

⌈then the people of the Geats made ready for him a splendid pyre on the earth⌉ : one of the most moving ever written.[18]

After all, Tolkien explains that *Beowulf* is an artistically unified work and a heroic-elegiac poem through the knowledge of Christian poetry and the tradition of Anglo-Saxon poetics. His idea has had a considerable effect on modern studies of *Beowulf*.

The most important point is that we should read and appreciate the work according to the author's intention. It may be possible that the epic was composed by Tolkien's poet for Whitelock's audience.[19] Here we should perceive Charles Moorman's severe criticism of the Christian interpretation of *Beowulf*:

> I suspect that we have fallen into the habit of seeing *Beowulf* as a Christian poem simply because we know more about late medieval Christianity than we do about the Germanic paganism of the Dark Ages. It is far easier to look back at *Beowulf*, Church Fathers in hand, from the Christian vantage point of the late Middle Ages than from the pagan point of view of earlier centuries from which so little information has come down. ... Whitelock, for example, can be most explicit about the degree of Christian knowledge held by the poet's audience; she is, of necessity, silent concerning that same audience's knowledge of pagan doctrines.[20]

We should admit that we have just a little knowledge of the early middle ages. Especially before the conversion to Christianity, we know almost nothing about the Anglo-Saxons and their culture. We should be careful and we should not forget the fact that neither the age of Bede nor that of king Alfred the Great was the time of the *Beowulf*-composition.

In 1981, Karl Schneider gave a series of lectures on *Beowulf* in Sophia University, Japan. The lectures were got together and published in 1986. They were based on the Germanic cultural background, and they dealt mostly with pagan elements: the Scyld episode and the genealogy of the Scyldings, two cremation scenes, the features and the function of the Primary God, the Song of Creation, the belief in Youthful Brotherly Gods, the belief in *wyrd*, pagan ethics and so forth. Then he concludes on the Christian elements in *Beowulf* as follows:

(1) The mention of Cain and Abel (106 ff., 1261 f.)
(2) The concept of a *deus judex*, a judging God (181, 588 f.)
(3) The allusion to the Day of Judgement (974 ff.)
(4) The concept of the devil (101, 756, 786, 788, 1680, 1682, 2088 f.).[21]

This is what Schneider found as the Christian elements in *Beowulf*. From the viewpoint of the Christian elements, he was unique and radical. He never admitted any other

Christian elements, though this is not an article but a lecture, so that the description is not proved in full detail. He concluded his lecture with the following words:

> With this total view, the most difficult *Beowulf* problems can be understood, above all the most enigmatic, the Christian elements within the basically pagan epic. True, the view given is based on a number of assumptions, but there is no convincing proof ever to be reached with respect to a literary document of the past with which are connected as many problems as with *Beowulf*. The best that research can achieve is some degree of probability. And this, I think, has been achieved in the course of this seminar.[22]

For Schneider the Christianity in the Germanic work of art is nothing but a thin veneer on the Germanic cultural background: the Germanic paganism must have been camouflaged for the Christian church. On this point he is rather excessive in comparison with other *Beowulf*-scholars. The Christian church might not have necessarily abused the Germanic paganism. We should be careful to keep balance in our viewpoint.

However, we cannot read *Beowulf* without Schneider's works. For he is the only person who has appreciated the Germanic culture through the eyes of the ancient Germanic people.[23] Through his works we cannot know the Germanic paganism before the conversion to Christianity.

## Notes

1. George Clark, *Beowulf* (Boston: Twayne Publishers, 1990), p.3.
2. Clark, p.4.
3. Clark comments on Turner's editions: "The second (1807) and third (1820) editions revise and enlarge the selections from the poem." (p.4).
4. Clark, p.5.
5. Julius Zupitza, ed. *Beowulf* (Facsimile). 2nd ed., with new collotype photographs, introduction by Norman Davis. Early English Text Society, No.245 (London: Oxford University Press, 1959); Kemp Malone has published Thorkelin's transcripts and *The Nowell Codex*: Kemp Malone ed. *The Thorkelin Transcripts*. Early English Manuscripts in Facsimile, I(Copenhagen, Baltimore, and London: Rosenkilde and Bragger, 1951); Kemp Malone, ed. *The Nowell Codex*. Early English Manuscripts in Facsimile, XII. (Copenhagen, Baltimore, and London: Rosenkilde and Bragger, 1963).
6. Benjamin Thorpe, *The Anglo-Saxon Poems of Beowulf* (Oxford: Oxford University Press, 1855), pp.viii-ix.
7. Richard Wülker, *Geschichte der Englischen Literatur* (Leipzig und Wien: Bibliographisches Institute, 1900), p.25.
8. Wülker, p.22.
9. H.M. Chadwick, *Heroic Age* (New York: Cambridge University Press, 1912), pp.47-56; rpt. an Excerpt. in *An Anthology of Beowulf Criticism*. ed. Lewis E. Nicholson (Notre Dame, Ind.: University of Notre Dame Press, 1963), p.27; After Tolkien one of the most important studies is the work of Adrien Bonjour's *The Digressions in Beowulf*. Through his detailed investigation Bonjour made it clear that the epic was skillfully constructed from the intended digressions by the poet. Since the 19th century the 'digressions' in *Beowulf* are considered as the basis of the multiple authorship. However, through the study of Bonjour, it resulted that the digressions were not interpolations but

an intended technique of the poet.
10. W.P. Ker, *Epic and Romance* (London: MacMillan, 1931), p.160.
11. Frederick Klaeber, *Beowulf and the Fight at Finnsburg*, 3rd ed. (Lexington: D.C. Heath, 1950), pp.xlix-l; George Clark criticizes Klaeber's idea: "Klaeber's research was widely accepted as having demonstrated that Christianity permeates the language and texture of *Beowulf*, but his case depended on recognizing allusions and parallels to the Psalms, the liturgy, and the Gospels in the poem." (p.16); and he continues: "Klaeber thought the story ("a plot of mere fabulous adventures") required an allegorical gloss or Christian interpretation to match the "dignity" of its setting, but a compound of fantasy and realism has a positive appeal to postmoderns."(p.24).
12. Dorothy Whitelock, *The Audience of Beowulf* (Oxford: Clarendon Press, 1951), p.3.
13. Cf. Whitelock, p.11.
14. Whitelock, p.11.
15. Whitelock, pp.3-4; she continues: "It is not confined to a few —— or even to a number —— of pious ejaculations in the author's own person or in the mouths of his characters; an acceptance of the Christian order of things is implicit throughout the poem. It pervades the very imagery:" (p.4).
16. J.R.R. Tolkien, "Beowulf: The Monsters and the Critics." *Proceeding of the British Academy*, 22 (1936), pp.245-295; rpt. in *An Anthology of Beowulf Criticism*, pp.84-85.
17. Tolkien, pp.83-84.
18. Tolkien, p.85; In *Beowulf: The Poem and its Tradition* (Cambridge, Ma.: Harvard University Press, 1983), John D. Niles comments: "Forty five years ago, when J.R.R. Tolkien admitted *Beowulf* fully into the ranks of English literature with his eloquent address to the British Academy, he took the monsters as main point of reference. By respecting the marvelous in *Beowulf* rather than excusing it or wishing it away, he

succeeded better than anyone before him in discovering the source of the excellence of this excellent work." (p.4); George Clark, also; comments: "Tolkien's interpretation was less original than it seemed; his account of the poem was extremely selective and ultimately limiting, but his poetic gift, his rhetorical power, and his deftness in argument carried the day and his reading of *Beowulf* has entered the critical canon. Tolkien successfully defended *Beowulf* as a literary masterpiece and maintained that the poem's supposed defect —— the large role assigned to the monsters —— expressed a profound moral vision that establishes the poem's serious artistic merit."(p.9).

19. Clark, pp.14-15.
20. Charles Moorman, "The Essential Paganism of *Beowulf*," *Modern language Quarterly* 28 (1967), p.8.
21. Karl Schneider, *Sophia Lectures on Beowulf* (Tokyo: Taishukan, 1986), p.78.
22. Schneider, p.195.
23. For this matter see the more detailed discussion and representation in Karl Schneider, *Die germanischen Runennamen. Versuch einer Gesamtdeutung. Ein Beitrag zur idg./ germ. Religiongeschichte* (Meisenheim am Glan: Anton Hain K. G., 1956).

# Interpretation of the Line 2390b in *Beowulf*

The extant text of *Beowulf* has survived in just one copy of the manuscript. The history of the standard editions begins in the 19th century, since when many editions have been published to establish the standard. The number of *Beowulf* translation is numerous, as well. It is interesting to investigate the translations. The *Beowulf*-poet likes telling his story in an ambiguous manner, though it is natural for all Old English poets. Some phrase could have more than one sense, and so we must depend on many books of reference and criticism. One of the passages that are mysterious is line 2390: which may refer to both Onela and Beowulf himself.

One scholar translated the line as a passage in praise of Beowulf himself, but he does not provide any basis for his idea even in his Notes. In this paper we would like to investigate the passage through as many other translations in modern English as possible.

# I

The epic *Beowulf* itself has a long history, and it is full of mystery. The name of the author and the scribes are still unknown. The interpretation of the epic is filled with mystery: its cultural background is still in an enigmatic condition. Any line of the work could be Christian as Frederick Klaeber interpreted, and at the same time any lines could be pagan.

However, we would like to concentrate on the line 2390b. The situation around the line is confused. The Swedish king, Onela, was not the legitimate king, because he seems to have usurped the throne. He killed his brother Ohthere, and became king in the country of the Swedes. His nephews, Eanmund and Eadgils, escape from Onela to the Geatish land to which Beowulf belongs. Then the Geatish king, Heardred, accepts them. It was natural for the ancient Germanic people. So Onela attacks his nephews in Geatland and kills their protector, Heardred. At that time Weohstan, a Swede in Geatland, kills Eanmund on behalf of Onela. Then he goes back to his country, and Onela allows Beowulf to rule Geatland.

Later Eadgils returns to the Swedish country to kill his uncle, Onela, with arms and men provided by Beowulf. This is the beginning of Beowulf's reign in peace for 50 years.

## Interpretation of the Line 2390b in *Beowulf*

This is the situation of the context. This part of *Beowulf* text runs as follows:

|  |  |
|---|---|
|  | Him þæt tō mearce wearð; |
| hē þǣr [f]or feorme | feorhwunde hlēat, |
| sweordes swengum, | sunu Hygelāces; |
| ond him eft gewāt | Ongenðīoes bearn |
| hāmes nīosan, | syððan Heardrēd læg, |
| lēt ðone bregostōl | Bīowulf healdan, |
| Gēatum wealdan; | þæt wæs gōd cyning.¹ |

(ll. 2384b-2390)

|  |  |
|---|---|
|  | That was the end |
| for Hygelac's son, | when his hospitality |
| later earned him | a death-wound by sword, |
| and Ongentheow's son | turned about |
| once Heardred lay dead, | returned to his home, |
| let Beowulf hold | the royal chair |
| and rule the Geats. | He was a good king.² |

This is the scene in which Onela gives Beowulf the Geatish throne. From that moment, Onela leaves Beowulf and his nation untouched. The author says: "He was a good king." In this situation it is obvious that both Beowulf and Onela may be pointed out, or if this passage is interpreted in another way, it may be translated in ambiguous. Other translators regard this passage as neutral, as well. We would like to see examples in chronological order from the middle of the 19th century. The first example is that of Benjamin Thorpe. The text runs as follows:

> he þær orfeorme           he there fruitlessly
> feorh-wunde hleát, 4760   sank with *a* mortal wound,
> sweordes swengum,         with strokes of *the* sword,
> sunu Hygeláces;           *the* son of Hygelac;
> and him eft gewát         and again departed
> Ohtheres bearn,           Ohthere's son,
> hámes niósan,             *his* home to visit,
> syððan Heardred læg;      after Heardred had fall'n;
> let ðone brego-stol       *he* the royal seat left
> Beowulf healdan,          Beowulf to hold,
> Geátum wealdan:           over *the* Goths to rule:
> þæt wæs gód cyning. 4770  that was *a* good king.[3]
>
> (ll. 4759-4770)

It is well-known that Thorpe's edition has been obsolete for more than a century, though at least the line in which we are concerned is all right. Line 4770 in this text does not point out anyone else. Here is another translation by John Earle in the 19th century. The text runs as follows:

> That was the limit of his (Heardred's) career; he there for his hospitality got a deadly wound with dynt of sword, did Hygelac's son; and Ongentheow's (grand) son returned to draw to his home, when Heardred had

fallen; he let Beowulf possess the royal throne and reign over the Goths; —— that was a good king.

(ll. 2385-2391)[4]

Here again, like Thorpe, Earle translates Geats as Goths. Also Earle translates the last line "that was a good king"; it does not have any indication whether it is Onela or Beowulf. However, it sounds strange that Onela is regarded as Ongentheow's (grand) son. The works in the 19th century seem to be obsolete in our time.

William Morris also translated *Beowulf*. The text runs as follows:

> Unto him 'twas a life-mark;
> To him without food there was fated the life-wound,
> That Hygelac's son, by the swinging of swords;
> And him back departed Ongentheow's bairn,
> To go seek to his house, sithence Heardred lay dead,
> And let Beowulf hold the high seat of the king
> And wield there the Geats. Yea, good was that king.[5]

In this context the interpretation of "that king" is ambiguous. The translation is not a perfect one, but the text is better than that of Benjamin Thorpe. Morris was a better translator of *Beowulf*.

## II

In the early 20th century, the situation became better. The study of Old English became far advanced. The epic, *Beowulf*, became popular. John Clark Hall's translation is still estimated as a good one. The text runs as follows:

> So Hygelac's son came thus by his end,
> he had as his lot for harbouring them
> a murderous wound from the blows of a sword,
> and Ongentheow's son departed again
> to visit his home when Heardred lay low,
> but let Beowulf keep his place on the throne
> and govern the Geats; a good king was he![6]

(ll. 2384-2390)

This edition is the second impression in 1926. The first edition is published in 1914. There is another edition by the same translator, whose translation is highly estimated. Line 2390 says, "good king was he!" This line is neutral, because this sentence could mean both Beowulf and Onela.

Another translation in the early 20th century is by William Ellery Leonard. The text runs as follows:

> Heardred's end was that!

> For sheltering the rebels a mortal wound he gat
> By swinges of the sword-blade. And Bairn of Ongentheow
> Departed for to seek his home, at Heardred's over-throw,
> Leaving unto Beowulf the seat of ring-gívíng
> And Lordship over Geatmen — that was a goodly King![7]

This translation is quite a unique one. The translator interprets the work and has constructed it with his own words. It is a work of art produced by the translator. The text is not far from the original, but we cannot read and understand the original text better through this translation. It is all right as a story but we cannot say it is a faithful translation.

One of the best is J.R. Clark Hall's prose translation. The text runs as follows:

> That was his life's limit: he, son of Hygelac, in return for his hospitality, had as his lot a deadly wound by thrustings of the sword, and Ongentheow's son went back again to seek his home when Heardred lay low, and suffered Beowulf to occupy the throne and rule the Geats. He was a noble king![8]
> (ll. 2384-2390)

This is cited from the ninth edition published in 1980, though the first edition was published in 1911. Here again the translation is all right. Hall sometimes utilizes rather interesting expressions. His translation is accepted by great scholars and has been revised by C.L. Wrenn and J.R.R. Tolkien.

In 1949 there appeared another translation by Mary E. Waterhouse. The text runs as follows:

> That caused Heardred's end,
> When Hygelac's son, for hospitality,
> Received his death wound from the broadsword's stroke;
> And Onela, son of Ongentheow returned
> To seek his home after Heardred fell;
> But letting Beowulf possess the throne
> And rule the Geats; he was a good king.[9]
>
> (ll. 2384-2390)

In this context "good king" could be both Onela and Beowulf. The translator follows the author's ambiguous manner.

Now we turn to the case of Charles W. Kennedy in 1940. The text runs as follows:

> For harboring exiles
> The son of Hygelac died by the sword.
> Ongentheow's son, after Heardred was slain,
> Returned to his home, and Beowulf held
> The princely power and governed the Geats.
> He was a good king, grimly requiting
> In later days the death of his prince.[10]

Kennedy is the first scholar who translated "He" as Beowulf himself. To "requite" the death of his king was not Beowulf's intention. But it was natural for the ancient Germanics to support their guests. As a result Beowulf is obliged to take revenge against Onela: Beowulf supported Eadgils in his avenge. It was also an ancient Germanic law to avenge the murder of one's relations. After Beowulf, Wiglaf succeeds to the Geatish throne and his father killed Eadgils's brother on behalf of Onela. Eadgils will take revenge against Wiglaf. The cycle of feuds never ends. Kennedy's translation is not exact but explanatory.

On the other hand, David Wright in 1957 changed the passage as follows:

> This brought about the death of Heardred, whose hospitality earned him a mortal wound from the sword of Onela. After the death of Heardred, Onela withdrew to his own land and allowed Beowulf to occupy the throne and rule the Geats. He made an excellent king.[11]

Here it is ambiguous: the final sentence is neutral but this "He" sounds both Onela and Beowulf. It is rather hard to decide who "He" is.

Here is another translation by E. Talbot Donaldson. This translation has Old English text of *Beowulf*. It is not literal word for word translation but only prose translation. There are some other editions by Donaldson, whose texts are the same but do not have Old English text. The text runs as follows:

> For Heardred that became his life's limit: because of
> his hospitality there the son of Hygelac got his life's
> wound from strokes of a sword. And the son of
> Ongentheow went back to seek his home after Heardred
> lay dead, let Beowulf hold the royal throne, rule the
> Geats: that was a good king.[12]

In this translation we cannot find the translator's intention. In this context "that was a good king" sounds neutral. Donaldson's translation, though other editions do not have the original text, is the best. It seems to be better than Clark Hall's edition, because Donaldson is faithful to the original text.

Edwin Morgan (1967) translates the passage as follows:

> That was what brought him to the bounds of death;
> His own hospitality won him his wound,
> Won the son of Hygelac mortal sword-strokes.
> And Heardred once dead, the son of Ongentheow
> Turned back again to make for his home,
> Leaving Beowulf to guard the throne
> And rule over the Geats: a king worth the name![13]

This is also a free translation. In this case again, "a king worth the name!" is neutral. The sentence may point out both Beowulf and Onela. The story is all right but this is far from the original "context".

In 1967 another translation was published. Constance B. Hieatt put the original text into Modern English in an orthodox manner.

The text runs as follows:

> That caused the end of Heardred's life; the son of Hygelac gained nothing but a mortal wound. When Heardred lay dead, Onela went back to his own country, and let Beowulf hold the throne and rule the Geats. He was a good king.[14]

Hieatt seems to be accepted widely, because this edition was revised and enlarged later in 1982.

Here is another translation by G.N. Garmonsway (1968), revised in 1982. This book is famous for its notes on the ancient Germanic heroes in mediaeval literature. The text runs as follows:

> It was this that set a term to Heardred's life, for it was the lot of Hygelac's son to receive a deadly wound by strokes of the sword in return for this hospitality. And when Heardred lay dead, Onela, the son of Ongentheow, turned back to seek his home again, and let Beowulf hold the princely throne and rule the Geats — a fine king was he![15]

The context is neutral, though the subject in the final

sentence seems to indicate Onela. This translation is also close to the original text.

There is another translation by Michael Alexander. The text runs as follows:

> This led to the end
> of Hygelac's son; his hospitality
> cost him a weapon-thrust and a wound to the life.
> Ongentheow's son, Onela, turned
> to seek his home again once Heardred was dead;
> the gift-stool and the ruling of the Geat people
> he left to Beowulf; who was a brave king,
> and kept it before his mind to requite his lord's death.[16]

In this context "brave king" should be ambiguous, as previously noted, but Alexander continues "and kept it before his mind to requite his lord's death". The *Beowulf*-poet does not say anything about that. Through this translation we cannot appreciate the epic or will misunderstand the epic.

The next one is a German translation. This edition by Gerhard Nickel(1976) has the original text and a German translation. The text runs as follows:

> Dies bedeutete das Ende seines Lebens. Für seine Gastfreundschaft erhielt Higelacs Sohn von Schwerthieben eine tödliche Wunde, und Ongentheows Sohn kehrte, als Heardred tot war, in seine Heimat zurück und ließ

Beowulf den Thron besteigen und die Gauten regieren.
Er war ein guter König![17]

In this context, this "Er" seems to signify Onela rather than Beowulf, though the context is neutral again. Since 1950 scholars and translators seem to follow Klaeber's original text edition.

Another German translation is Felix Genzmer's text (1953). This is the best in the case of the German translation, though it does not have the original text. The translation runs as follows:

> Das geriet ihm zum Tod:
> für das Obdach erhielt / Hygelaks Erbwart,
> getroffen vom Schwert, / die Todeswunde,
> und Ongentheows Erbe / machte sich auf,
> die Heimat zu genießen, / als Hardred gefallen.
> Beowulf ließ er / den Burgsitz halten,
> der Gauten walten. / Das war ein guter König.[18]

The final sentence seems to signify Onela, as well, but the context is neutral, again. This edition is widely accepted, not because it is inexpensive Reclam Geschen but because it is a good translation. The German translations, though we have seen just two examples, seem to regard the final sentence as signifying Onela.

In Everyman's Library we have R.K. Gordon's translation

(1926).
The text runs as follows:

> That ended his life. Deadly wounds from sword slashes he, the son of Hygelac, gained there for his hospitality; and the son of Ongentheow departed again to seek his home when Heardred was laid low; he let Beowulf hold the throne, rule over the Geats. That was a good king.[19]

This translation faithfully follows the original text of *Beowulf*, not only in words but also in the structure of the sentences. Gordon is a great scholar.

Next runs Michael Swanton's text (1978) as follows:

> That was to mark his end; because of his hospitality, Hygelac's son received a mortal wound by strokes from a sword. And when Heardred lay dead, Ongentheow's son went back to seek his home again — allowed Beowulf to hold the princely throne, rule the Geats. That was a great king![20]

This prose translation has the OE text and also follows the Old English text.

Another translation in Everyman's Library is published in 1982, translated by S.A.J. Bradley. The text runs as follows:

It proved to be the end of Heardred; for this hospitality Hygelac's son incurred a mortal wound from the blows of a sword, and when Heardred lay dead Ongentheow's son, Onela, set off again to make his way home, and left Beowulf to hold the royal throne and rule the Geats. He was a good king.[21]

This "He" is also neutral. The context of the interpretation is neutral, as well.

Another edition in 1982 is from the Oxford Classics, translated by Kevin Crossley-Holland. The text runs as follows:

> By receiving them,
> Heardred rationed the days of his life;
> in return for his hospitality, Hygelac's son
> was mortally wounded, slashed by swords.
> Once Heardred lay lifeless in the dust,
> Onela, son of Ongentheow, sailed home again;
> he allowed Beowulf to inherit the throne
> and rule the Geats; he was a noble king![22]

This is translated with the translator's own manner. The text sounds different in some phrases, though the last phrase is all right.

We have another translation by John Porter, first published in 1984. We have a reprint in 1988. John Porter comes out later with his clumsy translation in 1991. However, this edition is represented in simple English. The text runs as follows:

> Heardred, Hygelac's son,
> paid for his hospitality with his life's end,
> the death-wound dealt by a swung sword;
> and Onela, Ongentheow's son, returned
> home as soon as Heardred lay dead,
> leaving Beowulf to rule the Geats
> and guard their throne; this was a good king.[23]

In this context, the last sentence sounds neutral. However, if we take "this" as "the latter", the last sentence should be "Beowulf was a good king." This sounds like translator's technique which makes the translation more interesting.

Ruth P.M. Lehman (1988) translated this part as follows:

|  |  |
|---|---|
|  | He was marked for death |
| when for that friendship | by a fatal wound |
| from a brandished blade | the boy-prince perished. |
| Ongentheow's offspring, | Onela departed, |
| heading homeward | after Heardred's death; |
| that kingly Beowulf | might then claim the throne |
| and so guide the Geats. | He was a good ruler![24] |

This translation regards "He" as Beowulf, or this "He"

might be Onela. Then this edition does not have the original text. A translation printed side by side with the original text cannot be adventurous like this translation. This edition is a good one.

Another example is given by Barry Thraud (1990). The text runs as follows:

> When Heardred gave hospitality to the outcasts, he brought about his own death: For Onela, the most powerful lord among the Scylfings, slew Heardred with his sword. After Onela departed, Beowulf was left to rule over the Geats. He made a noble king.[25]

This is ambiguous again. In this context the last sentence could be both "Onela made a noble king" and "Beowulf made a noble king." The translation text is not an exact one but this part is all right.

The final example is the edition by John Porter (1991) who translates the text as follows:

>                              For Heardred it as end came;
> he there for hospitality     death-wound received
> from sword's strokes,        son of Hygelac;
> and back went                Ongentheow's son
> home to seek,                when Heardred lay dead,
> let the royal-seat           Beowulf hold,
> Geats to rule;               that was good king.[26]

This is also a translation printed side by side with the original text, but it is too clumsy. In the last line, we cannot find even an article, because John Porter seems to have wanted to follow the *Beowulf*-poet by translating the Old English text in a clumsy manner like the original text. This is exactly "literal word-by-word translation." The comments by other scholars are rather severe.[27] Porter reached too far, then his work became rather dull. This translation will be of some help to appreciate this epic-masterpiece but in some senses.

On this passage we cannot find any comment in any reference book except that of Howell D.Chickering, Jr. He has given a voluminous comment with his translation that is useful and applicable. He comments as follows:

> A textual point oddly related to the question of kingship: "that was a good king" 2390b. This is a prime example of the free-floating half-line, grammatically unconnected to its surroundings. It could be that Onela is good, since he lets Beowulf rule the Geats; most critics have thought so. The half-line concludes a sentence that started at 2386 with Onela as the main subject. Yet Beowulf is a good king too, and elsewhere in the poem there are sudden shifts of reference across the caesura. Perhaps Beowulf is to be contrasted with Onela. Unlike Onela, who twice invaded Geatland, Beowulf makes no feuding raids as a king. But we have no grammatical way of knowing this was intended.

When the diction is as fully formulaic as this half line, Old English poetic style will often lack particularity of reference. When the poet is not particular, the reader cannot be.[28]

Since line 2390b is neutral, it could mean both Beowulf and Onela. Almost all scholars and translators as we have seen already regard as neutral, except for two examples: Charles W. Kennedy and P.M. Lehman. On the other hand, David Wright probably considers "þæt" as Onela. Other translations, so far as we could survey them since 1855, seem to regard the subject of the line as neutral. As Chickering, Jr. concludes, the interpretation of line 2390b should be suspended.

## III

Now we have some Japanese translations of *Beowulf*. The oldest one is Fumio Kuriyagawa's work in 1940.[29] His interpretation of line 2390 is neutral. This is the first and the best translation in Japanese. There are other translations into Japanese: Sei Nagano,[30] Kinshiro Oshitari,[31] Takeichi Hazome,[32] and Kazuhiko Ogawa.[33] The first two are prose translations and the last two are translations in verse. Nagano's translation is so free that students cannot count on it, in reading the original text. Oshitari's text is much better, though there is a certain problem with line 2390. He translates "þæt" as Beowulf himself. Oshitari and Nagano do not give any explanation for their notes. As we have previously noted, the line should be regarded as ambiguous. Their translations are not acceptable. The fourth is Hazome's translation, which regards "þæt" as the Swedish king Onela. And Ogawa regards the line as ambiguous.

It is interesting that Japanese translations show variety, though two of the translators regard the line as referring to Beowulf himself. One regards "þæt" as Onela. Kuriyagawa's edition and Ogawa's edition are the only editions that take the line as neutral. The oldest one and the latest one are the best in this case. It is just a half line of the huge literary work of art. But even such a small part of the work reveals the appreciation of the translations. It is interesting that many of the translations depends on the translator's intention. It is strange that many Japanese scholars know the Old English grammar in detail, but some of them seem not to see the context. They seem to intend on making a new story of their own.

## Conclusion

We have seen the interpretations of line 2390 through specific texts. The *Beowulf*-poet is fond of presenting his text in an ambiguous manner. In stead of this research, the interpretation of line 2390 is still somewhat ambiguous. The line may represent both Onela and Beowulf, which is the obvious intention of the author. Translating the text with any exact name is not the best interpretation.

Most of the modern Japanese translations are not in use, even in the case that the translator is a famous scholar. We will have to be more careful. It is the limitation of a translation as well. If we translate some literary work, we should know not only the language itself but also the cultural background of the literary work of art.

Translation is not only the interpretation of a language but also the interpretation of a culture that is not known to the reader of the translation. We will have to understand the author himself with his cultural background, even his mind and heart at the moment of his work.

## Notes

1. Frederick Klaeber, ed. *Beowulf and The Fight At Finnsburg* (Boston: D.C. Heath, 1950), p.90.
2. Howell D. Chickering, Jr., trans. *Beowulf, A Dual Language Edition* (New York: Anchor Press, 1977), p.193.
3. Benjamin Thorpe, trans. *The Anglo-Saxon Poems of Beowulf, The Scôp or Gleeman's Tale, and The Fight at Finnesburg. with A Literal Translation, Notes, Glossary, Etc.* (Oxford: John Henry Parker, 1855), pp.160-161; *Beowulf Together with Widsith And The Fight At Finnesburg in the Benjamin Thorpe Transcription And Word-for-Word Translation With An Introduction By Vincent. F. Hopper* (New York:

Woodbury, 1962), pp.160-161.
4. John Earle, trans. *The Deeds of Beowulf An English Epic Of The Eighth Century Done Into Modern Prose* (Oxford: The Clarendon Press, 1892), p.78.
5. William Morris, trans. *The Collected Works Of William Morris With Introduction By His Daughter Mary Morris* Vol. x. *Three Northern Love Stories The Tale of Beowulf* (London: Longmans Green and Company, 1911), p.251.
6. John R. Clark Hall, trans. *Beowulf A Metrical Translation Into Modern English* (Cambridge: Cambridge University Press, 1926), p.86.
7. William Ellery Leonard, trans. *Beowulf A New Verse Translation For Fireside and Class Room* (New York: Appleton-Century-Crofts, 1923), p.102.
8. John R. Clark Hall, trans. *Beowulf And The Finnsburg Fragment A Translation Into Modern English Prose* ed. C. L. Wrenn and J.R.R. Tolkien (London: George Allen & Unwin, 1980), p.140.
9. Mary E. Waterhouse, trans. *Beowulf In Modern English A Translation in Blank Verse* (Cambridge: Bowes and Bowes, 1949), p.83.
10. Charles W. Kennedy, trans. *Beowulf The Oldest English Epic* (New York: Oxford University Press, 1962), p.77.
11. David Wright, trans. *Beowulf* (Harmonsworth: Penguin Books, 1964), p.83.
12. E. Talbot Donaldson, trans. *Beowulf* (New York: W.W. Norton, 1966), p.129.
13. Edwin Morgan, trans. *Beowulf* (Berkeley and Los Angels: University of California Press, 1967), p.65.
14. Constance B. Hieatt, trans. *Beowulf and Other Old English Poems* (New York: The Odyssey Press, 1967), p.70.
15. G.N. Garmonsway and Jacqueline Simpson, trans. *Beowulf and its Analogues* (London: J. M. Dent, 1980), p.63.
16. Michael Alexander, trans. *Beowulf* (Harmonsworth: Penguin Books,

1977), p.126.
17. Gerhard Neckel, trans. *Beowulf und Die kleineren Denkmäler Der Altenglischen Heldensage Waldere Und Finnsburg* (Heidelberg: Carl Winter, 1976), p.148.
18. Felix Genzmer, trans. *Beowulf Und Das Finnsburg-Bruckstück* (Stuttgart: Philipp Reclam, 1978), p.74; cf. Martim Lehnert translates as follows:

|  | Das war Heardreds Ende. |
| --- | --- |
| Wegen seiner Gastfreundschaft | erhielt er dort eine gefährliche Todeswunde |
| Durch schwerthiebe, | der schwache Sohn Hygelacs, |
| Und Ongentheows Sohn | kehrte eilends zurück |
| In sein Heimatland, | nachdem Heardred gefallen war. |
| Damit wurde Beowulf | zum Gebieter des Landes, |
| Zum Herrscher über die Gauten. | Das war ein guter König! |

Martin Lehnert, trans. *Beowulf Ein altenglisches Heldenepos Übertragen und herausgegeben* (Leipzig: Insel-Verlag, 1986), pp.103-104.
19. R.K. Gordon, trans. *Anglo-Saxon Poetry* (New York: J.M. Dent, 1977), p.48.
20. Michael Swanton, trans. *Beowulf* (Manchester: Manchester University Press, 1978), p.149.
21. S.A.J. Bradley, trans. *Anglo-Saxon Poetry* (London: J.M. Dent, 1987), p.474.
22. Kevin Crossley-Holland, ed. and trans. *Anglo-Saxon World An Anthology* (Oxford: Oxford University Press, 1984), p.134.
23. John Porter, trans. *Beowulf* (Felinfach: Llanerch Enterprises, 1988), No Page.
24. Ruth P. M. Lehmann, trans. *Beowulf An Imitative Translation* (Austin: University of Texas Press, 1988), pp.85-86.
25. Barry Tharaud, trans. *Beowulf* (Colorado: University Press of

Colorado, 1990), p.140.
26. John Porter, trans. *Beowulf Text And Translation* (Norfolk: Anglo-Saxon Books, 1995), p.145; cf. Seamus Heaney translates as follows:

> That marked the end
> for Hygelac's son : his hospitality
> was mortally rewarded with wounds from a sword.
> Heardred lay slaughtered and Onela returned
> to the land of Sweden, leaving Beowulf
> to ascend the throne, to sit in majesty
> and rule over the Geats. He was a good king.

Seamus Heaney, trans. *Beowulf A New Verse Translation* (New York: Farrar, Straus and Giroux, 2000), pp.161-163.

27. Douglas D. Short "Translations of *Beowulf*," in *Approaches to Teaching Beowulf*, ed. Jess B. Bessinger, Jr., and Robert F. Yeager (New York: The Modern Language Association of America, 1993), p.14.
28. Howell D. Chickering, Jr. ibid., p.365.
29. Fumio Kuriyagawa translates the passage as follows: "こは彼［ヘアルドレード］に取りて生命の終とぞなりにける。かれ、ヒュゲラークの息［ヘアルドレード］は其処にて、扶助の返報として、死の傷、剣の打撃をぞ得給ひしなる。而してヘアルドレード倒れ給ひてよりオンゲンセーオウの子［オネラ］は再び故国を訪れむとて帰り行けり。彼はベーオウルフをしてかの玉座を保ち、ゲーアタスを治めるに任せしなり。そは良き王に在しけり。"　厨川文夫『ベーオウルフ』（東京：岩波書店、1940), p.96.
30. Sei Nagano puts the passage as follows: "そのことはヘアルドレード王の死を招いた。せっかくの接待があだとなり、ヒュイェラークの子息なる彼は生命にかかわる傷を負うた。太刀にて撃たれることになった。そしてオンイェンゼーオウの子オネラは、ヘアルドレードが倒れ伏したる後、おのが家郷へ帰るべく旅立った。彼はベーオウルフに王位に即

くことを、イエーアト人らを治めることを容した。ベーオウルフは英明なる王であった。" 長埜盛『ベーオウルフ』(東京:吾妻書房、1966), pp.293-294.

31. Kinshiro Oshitari translates as follows: "それがヘアルドレード君の命取りとなった。ヒイェラーク公の子息は、客への手厚きもてなしの酬いとして死に至る深手を、剣の一撃を見舞われることとなったのである。ヘアルドレード君が斃れるや、オンゲンセーオウの子息オネラは国へと引き揚げ、ベーオウルフをして王位に就かしめ、イエーアト人を治めしめた。さても、ベーオウルフこそは優れたる王であった。" 忍足欣四郎『ベーオウルフ』(東京:岩波書店、1990), p.227.

32. Takeichi Hazome interprets the passage as follows: "それは彼には生命の終りとなった、ヒゲラークのみ子は彼らを保護したため剣の打撃によって致命傷を受けた。またヘアルドレードが逝った後、オンゲンセーオーの子は再び故国を訪れようと帰って行き、ベーオウルフが兵馬の権を司りゲーアタスを治めるのに任せた、実に立派な王であった。" 羽染竹一『古英詩大観』(東京:原書房、1985), p.82.

33. Kazuhiko Ogawa translates as follows: "そがかの君に死を呼びぬ。一臂仮したが仇となり命取りなる傷負いぬ白刃風きる一撃で、ヒィエラークの親王は。そののち旅に立ちにけりオンゲンセーオゥの公達は古里の地を尋ねつつ、ヘアルドレード絶えしのち、王の位を許したりベーオウルフが有するを、イェーアト人を統べるのを。そは優れたる王なりぬ。" 小川和彦『ベーオウルフ』(東京:武蔵野書房、1993), pp.186-187.

# Epilogue

We have seen some aspects of the epic, *Beowulf*. My papers are my impressions about them at present. The epic has usually been regarded as a complete Christian poem with just some pagan elements as a spice. The poet and his audience might be Christians. Even though they were Christians of whatever date, they must have enjoyed pre-Christian, blood-thirsty, heroic stories. It is natural for the Anglo-Saxons in the early middle ages. They were not modern sophisticated people. The events in the epic were usual episodes in their everyday life. They lived between war and war. And they were surrounded by wild nature. Huge forests must have been thicker and darker in their age. Wild animals could be terrible monsters for them. In the wilderness they could see the Grendels and a dragon. We should keep their Zeitgeist in our mind. Or we should know their "heart and mind" to understand them better. It is difficult right now.

In my idea, the epic, *Beowulf*, is the time of transition from the pagan to the Christian age. In a sense the author might have wanted to provide his own Bible story with a

Germanic hero. In its long history Christianity has accepted pagan elements through the ages. Christianity and paganism have often been close to each other. Nowadays it is hard to tell Christianity from paganism. In this book some pagan elements have been indicated but we cannot know the whole aspect of the Germanic paganism in the age of the composition of the epic. In the case of *Beowulf* we cannot know the real intention of the author; we can just imagine what he thought.

In this book we have not seen the Celtic elements in *Beowulf*. The Celts are expressive and their myth and legends are more fruitful than the Germanic ones. They must have had great influence on Anglo-Saxon literature. The Celtic influences have long been suggested: we will rely on the Irish, Scottish, and Welsh literary tradition and their archaeological discoveries. They are still under study; it is to be hoped that we may yet discover unprinted manuscripts and documents that have not been regarded by the most scholars. We will come to learn more about Old English and in particular about its culture and archaeological backgrounds. And we will have to parallel Christian-Latin texts. Cynewulf and his school may be suggested as examples. The Anglo-Saxons and Celts in Britain have already had the tradition of Latin school culture before the 10th century.

Tacitus' *Germania* should be a Bible for the study of early Anglo-Saxon and Germanic cultures. It has, unfortunately, been disregarded. But we should remember it is a contemporary document for Germanic culture. It is a first hand document by a Roman writer, even though he had never been to Germania. It is the first printed source for Germanic culture. We should never forget the importance of his work, when we talk about their culture. It will shed light on our extant questions. And in future we will have answers for them.

# Selected Bibliography

**Alexander, Michael.** trans. *Beowulf.* Harmonsworth: Penguin, 1977.

———. *Old English Literature.* London: The MacMillan Press, 1983.

**Allen, Michael J.B. and Calder, Daniel G.** trans *Sources and Analogues of Old English Poetry.* Cambridge: D.S. Brewer, 1976.

**Arent, A. Margaret.** "The Heroic Pattern: Old Germanic Helmets, Beowulf and Grettis saga." *Old Norse Literature and Mythology: A Symposium.* ed. Edgar C. Polomé. Austin: University of Texas, 1969, 130-199.

**Bennett, J.A.W.** *Middle English Literature.* Oxford: Clarendon Press, 1986.

**Benson, Larry D.** "The Pagan Coloring of Beowulf." *Old English Poetry: Fifteen Essays.* ed. Robert P. Creed. Providence: Brown University Press, 1967, 193-213.

**Bentinck Smith, M.** "Old English Christian Poetry." *The Cambridge History of English Literature,* vol. I Ed. Sir A.W. Ward and A.R. Waller. Thetford, Norfolk: Cambridge University Press, 1974, 41-64.

**Blair, P. Hunter.** *An Introduction to Anglo-Saxon England.* Cambridge: Cambridge University Press, 1977.

**Bliss, A.J.** *The Metre of Beowulf.* Oxford: Blackwell, 1958.

**Bloom, Harold.** ed. *Beowulf, Modern Critical Interpretations.* New York: Chelsea House Publishers, 1987.

**Bolton, W.F.** *Alcuin and Beowulf.* New Brunswick, NJ: Rutgers University Press, 1978.

**Bonjour, Adrien.** *The Digressions in Beowulf.* Oxford: Blackwell, 1970.

**Bradley, S.A.J.** *Anglo-Saxon Poetry.* London: Dent, Everyman's Library, 1982.

**Branston, Brian.** *Gods of The North.* London: Thames and Hudson, 1980.

**Brodeur, Arthur G.** *The Art of Beowulf.* Berkeley: University of California Press, 1971.

**Brønsted, Johannes.** *The Vikings.* trans. Kalle Skov. Harmonsworth:

Penguin, 1978.

Caie, Graham D. *Beowulf, York Notes*. Hong Kong: Longman, York Press, 1984.

Chadwick, H. Munro. "Early National Poetry." *The Cambridge History of English Literature*, vol. I. ed. Sir A.W. Ward and A.R. Waller. Thetford, Norfolk: Cambridge University Press, 1974, 19-40.

——————. *The Heroic Age*. New York: Cambridge University Press, 1912, 47-56. Rept. an Excerpt. *An Anthology of Beowulf Criticism*. Ed. Lewis E. Nicholson. Notre Dame, Ind.: University of Notre Dame Press, 1980, 23-33.

Chadwick, Nora. *The Celts*. Harmonsworth: Penguin, 1970.

Chambers, R.W. *Beowulf: An Introduction to the Study of the Poem* with a Discussion of the Stories of Offa and Finn. 3rd ed., with Supplement by C.L. Wrenn. London: Cambridge University Press, 1959.

——————. ed. *Beowulf with Finnsburg Fragment*. Revised by A.J. Wyatt. Cambridge: Cambridge University Press, 1948.

Chance, Jane. *Woman as Hero in Old English Literature*. New York: Syracuse University Press, 1986.

Chickering, Jr. Howell D. *Beowulf, A Dual-Language Edition*. New York: Doubleday, 1977.

Clark, George. *Beowulf*. Boston: Twayne Publishers, 1990.

Creed, Robert Payson. *Reconstructing the Rhythm of Beowulf*. Columbia, Mo: University of Missouri Press, 1990.

Curtius, Ernst Robert. *European Literature and Latin Middle Ages*. trans. Willard Trask. New York: Princeton University Press, 1973.

Damico, Helen. *Beowulf's Wealhtheow and the Valkyrie Tradition*. Madison: University of Wisconsin Press, 1984.

Davidson, Hilda R. Ellis. *The Sword in Anglo-Saxon England*. Oxford: Clarendon Press, 1962.

——————. *Gods and Myths of Northern Europe*. Baltimore: Penguin,

1976.

———. *Myth and Symbols in Pagan Europe*. New York: Syracuse University Press, 1988.

———. "The Hill of the Dragon: Anglo-Saxon Burial Mounds in Literature and Archaeology." Folk-Lore 61 (1950), 169-185.

**Dobbie, Elliott van Kirk.** ed. *Beowulf and Judith. The Anglo-Saxon Poetic Records*, IV. New York: Columbia University Press, 1953.

———. ed. *The Anglo-Saxon Minor Poems*. The Anglo-Saxon Poetic Records, VI. New York: Columbia University Press, 1942.

**Du Bois, Arthur E.,** "The Dragon in *Beowulf*", *PMLA*, 72 (1957), 819-22

**Dumézil, Georges.** *Gods of the Ancient Northmen*. ed. Einar Haugen. Berkeley: University of California Press, 1977.

**Earle, John and Plummer, Charles.** *Two of the Saxon Chronicles Parallel*. Oxford: Clarendon Press, 1929.

**Eliason, Norman E.** "The "Thryth-Offa Digression" in *Beowulf*", *Medieval and Linguistic Studies in Honor of Francis Peabody Magoun, Jr.*, ed. Jess B. Bessinger, Jr., and Robert P. Creed. New York: New York University Press, 1965.

**Elliott, R.W.V.** *Runes, an Introduction*. Manchester: Manchester University Press, 1971.

**Fry, Donald K.** ed. *Finnsburh Fragment and Episode*. London: Methuen, 1974.

**Garmonsway, G.N., Jacquline Simpson, and Davidson, Hilda Ellis.** *Beowulf and its Analogues*. London: Dent, 1980.

**Genzmer, Felix.,** trans. *Beowulf und das Finnsburg-Bruchstück*. Stuttgart: Philipp Reclam Jun., 1978.

**Girvan, Ritchie.** *Beowulf and The Seventh Century: Language and Content*. London: Methuen, 1971.

**Goldsmith, Margaret E.** "The Christian Perspective in *Beowulf*", Comparative Literature, 14 (1962), 71-80; rpt. in *Nicholson Anthology*, 373-386.

———. *The Mode and Meaning of Beowulf*. London: Athlone Press,

1970.

**Gordon, Eric V.** *An Introduction to Old Norse.* Oxford: Clarendon Press, 1974.

**Hall, John R. Clark.** *A Concise Anglo-Saxon Dictionary.* 4th ed., with a supplement by Herbert D. Meritt. New York: Cambridge University Press, 1975.

——————. trans. *Beowulf, A Metrical Translation into Modern English.* Cambridge: Cambridge University Press, 1926.

**Halsall, Maureen.** *The Old English Rune Poem: a critical edition.* Toronto: University of Toronto Press, 1981.

**Haugen, Einar.** *The Scandinavian Languages.* London: Faber and Faber Limited, 1976.

**Heaney, Seamus., trans.** *Beowulf. A New Verse Translation.* New York: Farrar, Straus and Giroux, 2000.

**Henry, P.L.** *The Early English and Celtic Lyric.* London: George Allen & Unwin, 1966.

**Hill, John M.** *The Cultural World in Beowulf.* Toronto: University of Toronto Press, 1995.

**Holthausen, F.** ed. *Beowulf,* 2 vols. Heidelberg: Carl Winter, 1921.

**Hoops, Johannes.** *Kommentar zum Beowulf.* 1932; rpt. Heidelberg: Carl Winter, 1965.

**Irving, Edward B., Jr.** *A Reading of Beowulf.* New Haven and London: Yale University Press, 1968.

——————. *Rereading Beowulf.* Philadelphia: University of Pennsylvania Press, 1989.

**Jones, Gwyn.** *Kings Beasts & Heroes.* London: O.U.P., 1972.

**Kellner, Leon.** *Historical Outlines of English Syntax.* London: MacMillan, 1913.

**Ker, W.P.** *Epic and Romance.* London: MacMillan, 1931.

——————. *The Dark Ages.* London: Blackwood, 1911.

**Klaeber, Frederick.** ed. *Beowulf and the Fight at Finnsburg.* 3rd ed.,

Lexington: D.C. Heath, 1950.

──────. "Die christlichen Elemente im *Beowulf*," *Anglia* 35 (1911), 111-36, 249-70, 453-82; *Anglia* 36 (1912), 169-199.

Lawrence, William Witherle, "The Dragon and His Lair in *Beowulf*", *PMLA*, 33 (1918), pp.547-583.

──────. *Beowulf and Epic Tradition*. Cambridge, MA: Harvard University Press, 1930.

Lockwood, W.B. *Languages of the British Isles Past and Present.* London: Andre Deutsch, 1975.

Macrae-Gibson, O.D., ed. *The Old English Riming Poem.* Cambridge: D.S. Brewer, 1983.

Malone, Kemp. "Beowulf", *English Studies* 29 (1948), 161-172: rpt. in *Nicholson Anthology*, 137-154.

McNamee, M.B. S.J. "Beowulf - An Allegory of Salvation?" *Journal of English and Germanic Philology*, 59 (1960), 190-207: rept. in *Nicholson Anthology*, 331-352.

Mitchell, Bruce & Robinson, Fred C. *A Guide to Old English.* Oxford: Blackwell, 1982.

Mitchell, Bruce. *Old English Syntax*, 2 vols. Oxford: Clarendon Press, 1985.

Moorman, Charles. "The Essential Paganism of *Beowulf*," *Modern Language Quarterly* 28 (1967), 3-18.

Nelson, Marie. *Structures of Opposition in Old English Poems.* Amsterdam: Rodpi B.V., 1989.

Nicholson, Lewis E., ed. *An Anthology of Beowulf Criticism.* Notre Dame, Ind.: University of Notre Dame Press, 1980.

Nickel, Gerhard., trans. *Beowulf und die kleineren Denkmäler der altenglischen Heldensage.* Heidelberg: Carl Winter, 1976.

Niles, John D. *Beowulf: The Poem and Its Tradition.* Cambridge: Harvard University Press, 1983.

Orchard, Andy. *A Critical Companion to Beowulf.* Cambridge: D.S. Brewer, 2004.

Overing, Gillian R. *Language, Sign, and Gender in Beowulf.* Carbondale and Edwardsville: Southern Illinois University Press, 1990.

Puhvel, Martin. *Beowulf and Celtic Tradition.* Ontario: Wilfrid Laurier University Press. 1979.

Raw, Barbara C. *The Art and Background of Old English Poetry.* London: Edward Arnold, 1978.

Robinson, Fred C. *Beowulf and the Appositive Style.* Knoxville: University of Tennessee Press, 1985.

Saxo Grammaticus. *Saxo Grammaticus.* trans. Peter Fisher. Ed. Hilda Ellis Davidson. Suffolk: Brewer, 1979.

Schneider, Karl. *Die Germanischen Runennamen. Versuch einer Gesamtdeutung. Ein Beitrag zur idg./germ. Kultur- und Religionsgeschichte.* Meisenheim am Glan: Anton Hain K.G., 1956.

———. *Sophia Lectures on Beowulf.* Tokyo: Taishukan, 1986.

Schubel, Friedrich. *Probleme der Beowulf-Forshung.* Erträge der Forshung, 122. Darmstadt: Wissenschaftliche Buchgesellschaft, 1979.

Schücking, Levin L. "Das Königsideal im *Beowulf*". *MHRA* Bulletin 3 (1929), 143-54: rpt. and trans. as "The ideal of kingship in *Beowulf*." In *Nicholson Anthology*, 35-49.

Sedgefield, W.J. *Beowulf.* Manchester: University of Manchester Press, 1935.

Shippey, T.A. *Beowulf.* London: Edward Arnold, 1978.

Shippey, T.A and Haarder, Andreas. Ed. *Beowulf: The Critical Heritage.* London and New York: Routledge, 1998.

Sisam, Kenneth, "Beowulf's Fight with the Dragon," *Review of English Studies*, n.s. 9 (1958), pp.129-140.

———. *The Structure of Beowulf.* Oxford: Clarendon Press, 1966.

———. *Studies in the History of Old English Literature.* Oxford: Clarendon Press, 1967.

Stanley, E.G. "The Search for Anglo-Saxon Paganism." *Notes and Quarterly* XI (1964), 204-209, 242-250, 282-287, 324-331, 455-463, and XII (1965), 9-17, 203-207, 285-293, 322-327.

Ström, Folke. *Nordisk Hedendom*. Trans. Kunishiro Sugawara. Kyoto: Jinbun Shoin, 1982.

Tacitus, Publicius Cornelius. *Germania*. London: William Heinemann, 1980.

Taniguchi, Yukio., trans. Edda. Ed. V.G. Neckel & H. Kuhn, A. Holtmark & J. Helgason. Tokyo: Shincho-sha, 1973.

Thorpe, Benjamin. *The Anglo-Saxon Poems of Beowulf, The Scôp or Gleeman's Tale, and The Fight at Finnesburg with A Literal Translation, Notes, Glossary, Etc.* Oxford: Oxford University Press, 1855.

——————. *Beowulf together with Widsith and The Fight at Finnesburg in the Benjamin Thorpe Transcription and Word-for-Word Translation with an Introduction by Vincent F. Hopper*. New York: Woodbury, 1962.

Tolkien, J.R.R. "Beowulf: The Monsters and the Critics." Proceedings of the British Academy, 22 (1936), 245-295: rpt. *Nicholson Anthology*, 51-103.

Wardale, E.E. *Chapters on Old English Literature*. London: Routledge & Kegan Paul, 1965.

Whallon, William. "The Christianity of *Beowulf*." *Modern Philology* 60 (1962/83), 81-94.

Whitelock, Dorothy. *The Beginnings of English Society*. The Pelican History of England, vol. 2. Baltimore: Penguin, 1981.

——————. *The Audience of Beowulf*. Oxford: Clarendon Press, 1951.

Williams, David. *Cain and Beowulf: A Study in Secular Allegory*. Toronto: University of Toronto Press, 1982.

Wilson, David. *The Anglo-Saxons*. London: Penguin, 1978.

Wilson, David. M. *The Vikings and their Origins*. London: Thames and Hudson, 1989.

Wilson, R.M. *The Lost Literature of Medieval England*. New York: Cooper Square Publishers, 1969.

## Selected Bibliography

Wrenn, C.L. *A Study of Old English Literature*. London: Harrap, 1980.

Wülker, Richard. . *Grundriss zur Geschichte der Angelsächsischen Literatur. Mit einer Übersicht der Angelsächsischen Sprachwissenschaft*. Leipzig: Verlag von Veit & Comp. 1885.

――――――. *Geschichte der Englischen Literatur*. Leipzig und Wien: Bibliographisches Institut, 1900.

Wulfstan. *The Homilies of Wulfstan.*, ed. Dorothy Bethurum. Oxford: Oxford University Press, 1957.

Wyatt, Alfred J. ed. *Beowulf*. Revised by R.W. Charles. Cambridge: Cambridge University Press, 1914.

Yoshimura, Teiji. *Geruman Shinwa*. Tokyo: Yomiuri-Shinbunsha, 1972.

Zupitza, Julius. Ed. *Beowulf* (Facsimile). 2nd. ed., with new collotype photographs, introduction by Norman Davis. Early English Text Society, No. 245. New York: Oxford University Press, 1981.

**橋本修一**（はしもと・しゅういち）
1956年東京生まれ。上智大学大学院修了。千葉工科大学助教授。主要な論文に hlāf vs brēad: their semantic rivalry, in Soundings (1992) pp.141-157. など。

# Beopulf

2006 年 3 月 15 日初版発行

著者
**橋本修一**

発行者
**三浦衛**

発行
**春風社**

〒 220-0044
横浜市西区紅葉ケ丘 53
横浜市教育会館 3F
Tel 045-261-3168　Fax 045-261-3169
http://www.shumpu.com/
info@shumpu.com

装丁・レイアウト
**長田年伸**

印刷・製本
**株式会社シナノ**

---

©Shuichi Hashimoto 2006.　All rights reserved.　printed in Japan.
ISBN4-86110-060-7 C3098 ¥2000E